DREAM WEAVER

Roam, Book Three

Dez Schwartz

A NineStar Press Publication

Published by NineStar Press
P.O. Box 91792,
Albuquerque, New Mexico, 87199 USA.
www.ninestarpress.com

Dream Weaver

Printed in the USA
First Edition
April, 2020

Print ISBN: 978-1-951880-61-3

Also available in eBook, ISBN: 978-1-951880-99-6

Warning: This book contains scenes of violence.

For Alyse, Nick, and everyone who has been on this journey with these characters since the beginning. Thank you for all your love and support. And keep looking to the stars.

Ethan Roam has faced a lot of nightmarish challenges—finding out he's a sandman, falling in love with the man who once hunted him, and thwarting attacks from The Order of Azoth, a secret occult organization set on using his bloodline to conquer the universe by controlling immortality. And the battle is far from over.

To defeat The Order and its leader, Phantom, Ethan must first find the original Sandman and then bring the fight to the Dream World. Saving the universe might be too tall an order for one dream creature, but with the help of his friends and some Celestial beings with questionable motives, Ethan just might be able to weave a trap of surreal proportions.

Chapter One

The Misguided Travelers

"Maybe it's broken." Ethan Roam, the sandman, shook the orb as though giving the device the magic-eight-ball treatment would bring it pulsing back to life.

"It had better not be. Technical support doesn't exist for magical artifacts," Mercury said.

Unsuccessful at reviving the device, Ethan set the orb down on the flattened surface of a nearby stalagmite. "I'm surprised to say it, but I really wish Chris was here. If anyone could fix this, it would probably be him."

"The Sandman Orb doesn't need to be fixed. You're just a bad driver," Mercury, the former vampire, Dacey, who was now transformed into a celestial entity, chided. Guarded, he turned a one-eighty to view what little he could make out about their dark cavernous surroundings. This wasn't the first alien planet Ethan had transported them to. But without the Sandman Orb working to give them a proper idea of where they physically were, it was becoming the most foreboding.

"Well, it would help if I had the driver's manual," Ethan defended, referring to the Codex, which had been left behind in Grady Hunter's study during the battle with the Hunters of Azoth, forcing them all to escape to the Dream World. "My driving doesn't explain why the orb just stopped working all together."

"Of course, it does. You took a wrong turn into an uncharted dimension. You're off the grid, darling."

"Sorry I didn't pull over to ask for directions," Ethan snipped.

Before he could add anything else to his sarcastic rebuttal, Mercury grabbed his arm in a protective manner and whispered, "Hide the orb. We're not alone."

Ethan scooped the archaic device up and stowed the orb away inside his jacket's inner lining, thankful Grady had bestowed the hand-me-down to him. His boyfriend's wardrobe had all sorts of custom pockets and restraints for portable weaponry, which Ethan found to be more and more a necessity.

A cluster of glowing eyes appeared in the darkness, followed by the sound of grunts. Ethan released a pulse of glowing blue dream energy from his palm to light up the space. The alien animal let out an annoyed squawk. Now that Ethan could get a good peek at the creature, he wished he hadn't.

The alien matched the murky gray sediment of the walls around them and appeared just as bulky. Its long body reminded Ethan of a salamander, only several feet longer and the size of a large crocodile. Once its gaggle of eyes adjusted to the light, the creature used six legs to propel itself rapidly toward them.

"Ball play is over. Back to basics," Mercury instructed. Mercury had no reason to worry for his own life, seeing as he currently held the title of Death. Instead, he'd be more interested in protecting Ethan's.

Picking up on his meaning, Ethan opened a portal back to the Dream World. In the blink of an eye, he and Mercury left behind a confused, angry, and hungry alien life-form.

*

Luckily, Mercury noted, *Ethan has mastered the art of landing on his feet and not on his face when traveling between worlds.*

Mercury grinned his approval. "You're improving."

"Not nearly fast enough," Ethan reminded him, producing the orb once again. At least now they knew for certain the device wasn't broken since the orb glowed back to working order with the atmosphere of the Dream World to energize it. "And this thing is basically useless without the Codex."

"There's more than one way to navigate foreign waters. Might I refer you to the Age of Exploration?" Mercury patted him on the shoulder in encouragement.

"No need to ask if you had any luck. I see Vincent still isn't with you."

They turned to see Marcus von Rottal, the vampire, standing nearby, his hands casually resting in his pockets.

Mercury had reason to be wary of Marcus's extreme interest. They were all in limbo until they could find Vincent Roam, Ethan's father—the original Sandman. Unbeknownst to the others, Marcus was the reason for Vincent's disappearance. He'd pushed Vincent into a portal out of unfounded jealousy. Mercury had guarded their secret in order to protect Marcus. However, the truth seemed destined to come out. Especially if they were successful in finding Vincent alive. Mercury imagined Marcus would want to put all his efforts into doing whatever he could to prevent that from happening.

As long as Mercury had known him, Marcus had put his own interests above everyone else's. Nothing could stop him or deter him once he set his mind on something.

Mercury would have to play his hand very close to keep Marcus from interfering or suspecting he mistrusted his intentions. And as unrealistic as his desire was, a part of him also hoped the others never would know the truth. Regardless of everything which had transpired to drive them apart in the last century, and as much as he'd shed the coil of his past life as Dacey, Mercury still felt protective over him. Or at least responsible for him.

"Marcus, darling! I'm so glad you're here," he lied. "Would you be a doll and fetch Grady and perhaps even the portly fellow? What's his name again?"

"Arthur," Ethan helped.

Mercury snapped his fingers in confirmation. "Yes! I have an ever-growing list of questions needing answers from those bookish occultist blokes."

"Hunter wandered into the dream forest," Marcus informed them. He often referred to Grady by his surname to slight him. "I was quite hoping he'd lose himself in there, but I suppose I'll go fetch him out if I must. Must I?"

Mercury nodded.

Marcus pursed his lips in response before making his way into the fluorescent-hued woods surrounding them.

Knowing full well Ethan would question the need to interrogate the other men, Mercury went ahead and answered. "Who has read the *Mechanics of Sleep Travel* more times than anyone else, and even better, who helped write the damned thing?"

*

Grady Hunter knelt on the vibrant grass. Upon closer inspection, every blade filled with stars and planets, each appearing to be home to its own galaxy. He surveyed the vast expanse of surreal nature around him, every inch of this strange world similarly cosmic. He imagined if one had to try to explain what infinity looked like, then the landscape of the Dream World would be the perfect demonstration.

Parched, and feeling much the helpless human, he'd stopped for the stream that ran through the woods. Drinking the water would be either pointless or dangerous, but he hoped he could at least find some relief by wetting his throat. He gave the water a light test with his fingertips which produced an oily swirl, creating a similar rainbow effect. He sniffed his hand for signs of toxicity, but the substance didn't smell of anything at all really. *Perhaps*, he wondered, *it's because nothing here is technically real.*

"This is not the time for existential analysis, Alexander," he chided himself, utilizing his birth name, a habit he'd slipped into when lost in serious thought. Deciding the water's property to be nothing more than the substance of induced dreams, and, therefore, non-toxic, he scooped up the liquid in his hands and splashed it on his face to refresh himself and clear his mind.

Much to his dismay, his efforts weren't successful since a wearisome voice greeted him the first thing afterward. "If one cannot be existential in the Dream World then Romanticism was a waste of everyone's time. What a dreary protestant thought. You really must be losing hope."

The only one pretentious enough to say such a thing had to be Marcus. Grady frowned in annoyance. Wiping the water off on his slacks, he stood to address the Austrian vampire.

"As much as it pains me to say this, I'm glad we have a moment to speak alone." Grady walked up the shore to confront him.

"That makes one of us. I'm only here as an errand. Dacey—erm, *Mercury* is seeking your council."

"Well, that makes bringing the topic up even easier. He's who I wish to speak with you about."

"Spare me the speech, Hunter. I already know what you're going to say. In order to move forward as a team, you want me to know what you two shared was fleeting and meant nothing. You never loved him and vice versa. Am I correct? Fabulous. Now, let's go, and I have no problem with walking in silence." He turned to leave.

"While those things are very true, they aren't what I wanted to address exactly."

Marcus faced him again and waited for him to continue, though it appeared to pain him to do so.

"Your jealousy does shine like a beacon, but I have been wondering...why? You've known him longer than any of us. You've shared so much more with him. You know how he can be. So, why would you, with all your supernatural power, ever feel threatened by anyone? Let alone a mortal. He, obviously, still loves you as much as a vampire–or Death—can, I suppose. No one can take that away, or else they would have by now."

Marcus gave a small laugh riddled with annoyance. "You do love to flatter yourself. I've never considered you a *real* threat, Hunter. Love is not the problem between him and me. The problem is loyalty. Rather, a lack thereof."

"May I persuade you to elaborate? For the benefit of my complete understanding moving forward."

"Tell me. Is there anything you wouldn't do for the young dream traveler?"

"No. I love and trust Ethan with every fiber of my being," Grady answered in earnest.

"So, you would follow him blindly, no matter the situation?"

"Perhaps not blindly. But I would die for him if necessary."

Marcus sneered. "Poetic. But it does frame my point. You're completely, unquestionably loyal to him. Dacey never granted me such loyalty. He may love me more than anyone else, but he's incapable of sticking by my side when things take a turn for the worse. A flighty, fickle little bat. Dacey and I loved each other, but we never trusted each other. I used to think him a coward, but these sandmen have proven what he is. A traitor. An opportunist. And now I have no idea what to expect in those terms from this Mercury fellow he claims to have become."

"Sandmen? Yes, of course. You knew Vincent too." Grady wondered what Vincent must have done to make him feel such a way.

"Dacey talked about him?"

Cautious, Grady opted for the simple truth. "He mentioned him once, fleetingly."

"He knew him fleetingly as well. Didn't stop him from choosing a sandman over me then either. I understand he knew Ethan for a very short amount of time and then was willing to toss himself into oblivion for him. I beg the question, why? He's had a history of engaging in self-destructive behavior for men he's only just met."

"Have you ever considered his lack of faith had more to do with the leadership in your relationship than you specifically?" Grady proposed. "What I'm saying is, perhaps you should shift the power and see if he still remains...flighty."

"We've tried switching dominance before. I didn't like it." Marcus turned to leave again.

"Did you even give him a chance?" Grady pressed him. "I mean, really? Did you follow him without question like you expect for me to do right now, or did you try to take the reins back at every turn as you're also doing in this very moment?"

Marcus held his tongue.

"Maybe this time around, you let him lead, and see if you get any further. What have you got left to lose?" Grady suggested with care.

Marcus offered him a genuine smile for the first time. "I'm beginning to determine you unbearably sensible."

"Thank you."

His smile disappeared. "This doesn't make us friends."

"I'm relieved we've cleared that up." Grady offered his own smile.

Marcus seem to mull the matter over for a second and then gave a curt nod to indicate the subject settled. Thankful they'd opted for a silent journey, Grady followed at a respectful and comfortable stride length behind him.

*

Mercury's slow pacing may have given away his nervous concern, but he kept his tone even. "You must tell us everything you know about dream travel. Specifically, any methods which may be useful when used in conjunction with the Sandman Orb." Grady, Marcus, Benny, Karen Roam, and Dr. Arthur Ellis sat, weary at this point, in the comfort of Kit's den. The kitsune had been more than hospitable in opening her home and any resources she had to make them more comfortable. She opted for her humanoid form since it made them—aside from Benny the werehuahua, who seemed to enjoy meeting another shapeshifter—the most comfortable. Kit raised an eyebrow at Mercury's demand as she finished handing out a few snacks most of the group seemed reluctant to attempt eating.

"Shouldn't you be asking Marcus this question?" Grady glanced at Marcus with suspicion. "None of us had ever encountered or even heard of the orb until he arrived."

"So much for gentleman's truces," Marcus scoffed, but his tone implied partial jest. Grady smiled at him in return.

Mercury narrowed his eyes at their suspicious behavior.

Marcus rested a heated gaze on Mercury, surely to show his disapproval of the dangerous territory he opened with his line of questioning.

Mercury clarified, "What I mean is in all of the research and experiments with dream travel Vincent engaged in and wrote about, there must be something that would help us! Vincent traveled without the Codex and orb, did he not?"

"I suppose," Arthur said. "I'd never heard anything about these artifacts before, but he did travel subconscious worlds. In layman's terms, the realms of spirits, like this one. I know nothing of his ability to transport himself to other places in the physical multiverse."

"Well, Sandman could," Mercury enlightened them. "The orb should be a guidance system, but one which can be modified and with the ability to retrace one's steps. Part of its purpose is to house the only knowledge of

Phantom's location from when he was excommunicated. Only a sandman would ever be able to glean that knowledge. With the help of the Codex, of course. Which is what we need and is now in the hands of the Order. It's the key to understanding that guidance system."

"Essentially, the Codex is a user's manual. And I'm kind of lost without it," Ethan said, facing the group.

Standing by Mercury's side, Ethan made a rather striking leader. His sandman nature had ebbed glowing stardust through his veins since the moment they'd arrived in the Dream World. He was in his element, and he wore the fact well.

It didn't go unnoticed by Mercury that both Marcus's and Grady's jaws exhibited just the slightest clinch at the sight of their allegiance.

"I see your problem but I'm afraid we don't have an answer," Arthur spoke up. "As far as I know, Vincent had no knowledge of this orb or any Codex. I don't see how it would help in finding him if he never used them."

It would have been so simple to inform them Marcus and the orb were the catalysts for sending Vincent to wherever he now resided, but Mercury held his tongue. He wasn't ready to play that hand.

"Perhaps it wouldn't. Suppose he's lost in some dreamscape. I mean, if he were on a physical plane, then you'd think he would've been able to pop himself back onto Earth whenever he liked. Am I not correct?" Marcus reasoned. It was such a devilish trick of words, Mercury had to commend him.

"He might be right," Kit spoke up. "The idea is not unheard of for a celestial to get trapped in a spirit realm. Nothing would have willingly kept him from his family."

"Kit has to be right," Karen agreed.

Grady turned to Mercury. "You're Death. Are you not free to travel those planes?"

"I can only usher the journey of the dead and monitor those in imminent peril. I'm not without oversight," Mercury answered. "It wouldn't do to have Death traipsing through other's dominions. Something about the title is *suspect*. I blame the scythe."

"Well, at least then we can assume Vincent is neither dead nor in peril," Arthur said.

"Can you complain to higher management? Perhaps they can grant you temporary passage," Grady suggested. "Who oversees you?"

"In a sense, existence itself," he answered. "Darkness gave Death its shackles and I wouldn't even dare to implore her to free me of them. I'm not exactly on her list of favorites; she blames me most for this entire mess, let's not forget. Not to mention, the idea is a moot point since she disappeared to the ends of the cosmos an eternity ago."

Grady huffed in annoyance. "There *must* be someone who can help us. Someone who can access every spirit realm."

"If my fath—the Sandman created the orb to guide himself back from exiling Phantom then why would he even need a Codex? He wouldn't have had time to write it if he'd been banished to Earth so soon afterward like you said," Ethan considered. "So, who wrote the Codex, and why? Is there something you're not telling us?"

There are many things, but this is not one of them. "There is someone else. And while they have always acted as though they were on Sandman's side, I have to wonder."

"Well, who then?" Grady demanded a clear answer.

"Nightmare," Kit offered. She bit her bottom lip.

"Yes," Mercury concurred. "Nightmare helped Darkness and Dawn banish us. He'd been tasked with hiding the orb and, presumably, creating the Codex. There's no telling how much time he spent with the orb before doing so. He's the only non-sandman with the potential to understand the orb and powers similar enough to Sandman's."

"And where is he now?" Grady prodded.

"He's right here," Kit answered. "In the Dream World. But...Nightmare isolated himself long ago, only dealing with those he takes under his command," Kit explained. "I was born and raised under his control, and my appointment was to watch over Vincent whenever he came to the Dream World. Tasked to keep track of him. Until, I couldn't. When he disappeared, I was relieved of my duties, a great dishonor. Vincent had been assumed existence-less since Charon—Death at the time—couldn't trace him."

"Existence-less? What does that mean?" Ethan asked.

Kit took a steadying breath before explaining. "It's when the cosmos absorbs you and refuses to relinquish control. Imagine being sucked into a black hole and frozen there, never to die but never to really live again either. You're just stuck infinitely in a speck of space, in an endless loop of nothingness."

Everyone grew silent as they each imagined such a terrible fate.

Kit continued, "I didn't know what had really happened to Vincent. But I did know Ethan existed, and one day, like all *somnium viators*, he would follow in his father's footsteps and arrive in the Dream World. I imagined I would win my rank back from Nightmare with such a wonderful surprise. But then…"

"Yes, dear heart? Go on," Mercury encouraged once she'd trailed off. He had already read where her confession was headed, and he planned his own strategic moves in a hurry based on the information, but he knew the others would need things spelled out for them.

"I began to question his motives," she continued. "Nightmare never had dominion over Sandman when Sandman ruled the Dream World. And I started to suspect the only reason he wanted to keep watch over the *somnium viators* coming through was, in fact, to ensure the true Sandman never returned to reclaim his throne. There's a chance he wants to keep the power he's grown accustomed to and may view sandmen as a threat."

"*Or* he could have been in cahoots with Phantom all along," Mercury offered his alternative theory. "Celestial fuckery!"

"But you don't know that for a fact, right?" Ethan pointed out. Something in his tone indicated he'd been making his own strategic plans while Kit addressed them.

"Well, no. But now the hand has been played on the table, it's rather hard to imagine anything else," Mercury admitted.

"Imagine it anyway," Ethan countered. "We have no other options at this point, and we've already wasted enough time. Worst comes to worst, all us going there will let him know is that I'm *not* Sandman. I can't keep popping in and out of realms aimlessly while my friends and family sit here and starve. We have to go to Nightmare and see if he'll help me learn to use the orb without needing the Codex."

Benny, who had been eating Kit's snacks without much of a problem or care, froze midbite at the idea of facing such an imposing figure. "I'm fine staying, actually," he muttered in a half whisper.

"Rather for the better," Mercury approved. "You all should stay behind."

Grady stood. "Well, I'm not. Sitting here with my hands tied while Ethan's out there facing devil-only-knows-what is not what I signed up for. I'm supposed to be by his side protecting him."

"And what if we do find Vincent? We need Arthur to bridge the gap," Ethan reminded them. "Technically, he has no idea who any of the rest of us are."

Marcus challenged Mercury with another glare.

Mercury chortled, "Nightmare would rip the life from you all and send you into eternal hellscapes before you even had a chance to say boo at him. We'll have to face Vincent without Arthur and hope for the best. It'll do Ethan no good to babysit mortals, trust me. You're most helpful here."

Grady crossed his arms. "Doing what exactly?"

Mercury strained to think of an acceptable answer.

"That's what I thought." Grady clapped his hands together. "The rest can stay behind but I have only one mission in life now so I'm going. End of discussion."

Marcus stood. "If he's going then so am I."

"Great!" Mercury declared, sarcastic. "Would anyone else care to commit suicide? I'll spend half the night ushering souls to the Spirit World while Ethan becomes Nightmare's new plaything. Splendid plan, everyone. I'm so glad I consulted you all."

"If there's any bit of Dacey left in you, then I have a hard time believing you're not at least a little enthralled at the idea of a possible orgy of the dead featuring the lot of us whatever your brand of Hell is. Now stop whining Mercury, and let the fox lead the hunt." Marcus turned to Kit. "Where is this isolated king of yours? I haven't made a deadly house call to royalty in quite some time, and I find myself rather looking forward it."

Chapter Two

Bad Omens

The familiar haze of the crystal ball which usually offered generous help while scrying gave no indication anything could be seen today. Vivian Edwards took a deep breath to try to keep her efforts focused, but she grew frustrated, knowing she had already been deep in focus the entire time. Her abilities as a witch weren't the problem. The problem seemed to be there was absolutely nothing to be seen.

From the doorway, Thomas Strong broke her concentration. "Babe, are you still in here?"

The smokey spell dissipated from the ball, rendering the tool idle once more. Vivian tapped the screen of her phone to check the time. While Thomas was at work, she'd spent the entire day trying to use various locator spells to track down Grady with no luck. Her disappointment must have been apparent because he set the takeout dinner bag he'd been holding down and entered their guest bedroom, which served as her sanctuary since they never really planned on having overnight visitors.

"I can't find him," she replied with a strained voice.

"Maybe he's hiding." Thomas sat down beside her. "You said he knows how to ward off spells that would give away his location."

Vivian didn't try to mask her concerned frustration. "Not mine. I'm his backup plan. He always keeps a psychic door open for me just in case."

"Maybe he doesn't anymore," Thomas hazarded a guess. "You two aren't exactly...friends now."

Vivian pursed her lips at the stinging remark. His words may have been the truth, but she thought Thomas could at least be a bit more sympathetic. Friendship status aside, her intuition screamed at her. "I can't find any of them. Not even Benny. Something is definitely wrong."

"Take a moment, Viv. Don't immediately jump to the worst possible conclusion," Thomas said. "I mean, Grady's *modus operandi* is putting himself in ridiculously dangerous situations; peril is practically a hobby of his. I'm sure he already has whatever situation he might be in handled."

Vivian shook her head, solemn. "That nightmare I had was a vision; I *know* it. They need help, and we're somehow connected. I don't even think they're on the physical plane anymore."

"Excuse me? If it was a vision where we all die, then running toward the danger seems like the quickest way to meet that outcome. How exactly do you plan on helping them, especially if they're in some other realm?" Now Thomas seemed frustrated for different reasons. He'd hoped their move to another state would've meant the end of ever having to hear about or deal with Dr. Grady Hunter and his exploits ever again. "What if this vision is leading you to an early grave? Or, what if you find him, realize you were wrong, and you finally have to face him?"

Annoyed, Vivian blew out the candles on the table. "I'm not wrong. And not at least trying to help in order to save our own necks would be selfish and cowardly. If we find them and everything is fine, then facing him is worth looking like a fool. Atoning for my mistakes is a price I'll be glad to pay in order to know they're safe."

Thomas softened. "What happened that night wasn't your mistake, Viv. You were under supernatural influence. Which is why I'm wary of anything trying to pull you back to Shady Pines. Things have been so much better since we left there."

"Better for who?" Vivian challenged. "I'm going back, Thomas. I'll never be able to live with myself if anything happened to them and I had brushed off this warning. You can come with me or you can stay here. I won't blame you or be angry with you if you stay, but I would appreciate it if you'd just trust my judgment."

"Okay." He took her hand in his to show support. "I'll go with you. But promise me something. No matter what happens, when we're done there, you'll come back here with me. To *our* life."

"Of course," she agreed. "I just need peace of mind on this."

He gave her forehead a light kiss. "All right. Let's grab a few things, and we can go tonight."

*

Several hours later, the house loomed in front of them. A ghost-like structure. Vivian didn't need to utilize her senses to know something was wrong made obvious since half the windows were busted out of Grady's manor and all the wards, which usually protected the house, had been deactivated.

"Damn," Thomas muttered. Vivian didn't have a need to argue with him about the validity of her vision any longer.

She took a step forward on the cobblestone drive. Thomas reached over and grabbed her elbow to stop her. "How do we know it's safe to go in?"

"I can tell no one is in there," she explained. "No one alive, anyway."

She continued to the front door with Thomas following close by her side. As soon as they entered, they were met with a whirlwind of screams and a chilling breeze that rustled drapes and scattered loose leaves around them that had come in through the broken windows. The madness stopped as abrupt as it had begun. Vivian brushed her hair out of her face to see Agatha and John, the ghostly housekeepers, there to greet them.

"Oh, I'm so sorry about this, Miss!" Agatha apologized with haste. "We were worried you were intruders coming back to damage our poor house even more. How have you been? Would you like some tea?"

"That's quite all right, Agatha, and I'm afraid we don't have time for tea." The entire house seemed to be in shambles. "What happened here?"

John shook his head in disgust.

"Ohhh!" Agatha wailed. "Things have been awful, Miss! Just awful. I'll tell you all about it, but we should move to the study so you can see for yourself the damage they've done."

Vivian and Thomas shared curious glances but followed the apparitions down the hall and into the large room that housed Grady's most prized esoteric books and artifacts in a glorious collection. Or at least it once had. Now everything lay scattered, broken, and even burned. The aftermath of a war zone.

Agatha wailed again as though seeing the mess herself for the first time.

"They put a hole in the wall, but it's gone now," John stated, not sounding unnerved in the slightest.

"Who did this? Grady?" Vivian prodded, overlooking the damage. Thomas had knelt to inspect a peculiar smudge on the floor.

"Yes. And no." Agatha wrung her ghostly hands. "They were attacked! Intruders, ones possessing their own magic, broke through all of the wards."

Thomas identified the stain. "This is blood."

"Oh, I thought I'd gotten it all!" Agatha cried again. "I've been cleaning for days even though you can't tell by the looks of this mess."

"Where are they now?" Vivian asked, frantic. "Are they alive?"

"Yes, I believe so. At least some of them are." Agatha hung her head. "I'm afraid Grady's father perished in the battle. Ethan helped the rest escape to the Dream World."

Awestruck, Thomas said, "Seems like you were right about them not being on the physical plane anymore."

Vivian chose to take the high road and not point out she'd been right about more than just that.

"Who did Ethan take with him?" she asked Agatha instead.

"Well, Grady, of course. Karen, Benny, Arthur, and some vampire—my apologies, I forget his name. Grady's mage friend fought against the intruders too, but he didn't make it away safe with the others. The intruders captured him."

"What mage friend?" Vivian prodded. She knew Grady had a multitude of supernatural connections, but she was unfamiliar with any mages in Shady Pines. Male witches, yes. But they were all in covens. Mages tended to be solitary.

"Chris," Agatha answered. "Oh yes, I forgot you didn't know him. Grady hired him to take your place after you left."

Embarrassed, Vivian bit her lip. Thomas cast her an *I-told-you-so* glance. He was probably thinking if she'd stayed then she would be the one being held captive by murderers right now.

"You said you've been cleaning for days," Vivian clarified. "So this means this probably happened around the same time I had my vision. Was there a man, or a creature, with a black cloak here during the battle?"

Agatha tried her best to recall. "No, dear. I can't imagine I remember anyone like that."

Vivian frowned, certain Death's figure had been in her vision. But sometimes visions weren't easy to decipher.

"Well, if they're in the Dream World with Ethan then they should be safe," Thomas tried to console.

"For now, maybe but we don't know anything for certain," Vivian pointed out. "Who were these intruders, Agatha? Do you have any idea?"

"Everything happened so fast it was hard to keep track," Agatha admitted. While ghosts could be everlasting, their short-term memories were not. "But there were several of them, and they were after Ethan. I can't remember if Grady said they were alchemists or part of some cult...perhaps both."

"Great, so we have a cult of wizards out for blood." Thomas shook his head with disdain and muttered, "Thanks, Grady. I would expect no less."

Vivian sighed, taking stock of the situation. "I need to find a way to contact them in the Dream World. I'm sure these men won't stop their hunt for Ethan, and they'll be in just as much trouble the moment they return as they were when they left. Unless we can find a way to stop them ourselves."

"Whoa there Viv." Thomas held up his hands in an effort to halt her train of thought. "You're one witch and I'm...well, not. If Grady and a handful of other people were no match for these guys, then how do you expect us to be?"

"We don't have to do this alone. I can call in a favor," Vivian replied, her mind made up. "Besides, if someone has been kidnapped, then we need to find them and free them. And if that someone *is* a mage, then all the better for us."

Thomas grimaced. "I can't change your mind about this, can I?"

"No," Vivian answered.

Thomas slumped his shoulders. "Fine. Who owes you a favor?"

*

Chris Reed lifted himself up on the cot as his head began to clear. He'd been lying down with a massive headache, and the pain of many lacerations he'd endured as torture the moment he'd regained consciousness in his isolation cell. As solitary confinement goes, the room wasn't really so bad. He'd seen worse. The cell was akin to a modest efficiency apartment without privacy. The door was open-faced and barred, but the entirety of the room had been warded against any possible escape attempts.

The Hunters and, specifically, a man named Chase, who called himself the Legate of the Order of Azoth, had tormented him with an inquisition and series of tests hoping to glean any information from him about Ethan.

Thankfully, he was good at taking a beating and holding his tongue, even against spells that tried to draw the answers out of him. They'd let him live, though, which meant they believed he still knew something, and he expected they would be trying new methods on him again soon.

He groaned as he moved, and every inch of his body screamed at him.

Chase strode up to the door of his cell, cocky and well-groomed in a suit and tie. The pin he wore on his lapel, the traditional symbol of Mercury, glistened.

"He lives," Chase stated with an evil smirk. "How are you feeling? Well rested, I hope?"

"I could do with a few more pillows, and the mattress sucks. Definitely giving you guys a one-star rating on TripAdvisor," Chris quipped. He applied every ounce of effort he could to make it seem as though the whole ordeal had left him unfazed.

His acting worked. Chase pursed his lips, and his jaw clinched in an annoyed manner. He had obviously been hoping Chris would have caved and begun begging for his freedom by now.

Chase said flatly, "I'll be sure to fetch you a Serta later."

"Thanks, I appreciate that." Chris fluffed his pillow for added effect and lay back down, staring at the ceiling, mostly so he didn't have to keep looking at Chase's face, but also because the stress of the situation made his headache return with full force.

"Leisure time is over, mage. You have work to do."

"Look, I promise I don't know anything you don't already know." Chris closed his eyes. "Kill me if you want but you're wasting your time trying to wrestle any information out of me. There's nothing useful up here." He tapped his temple.

"On that note, we can agree," Chase sneered. "As much as I did enjoy taking out my aggression on you, I'm afraid torture methods are no longer necessary...for now. Instead, your services have been requested."

A fear worse than torment sparked in Chris, and he rolled his head over to grimace at Chase again, raising a cautious eyebrow. "What kind of services?"

"My, my. You are stupid." Chase sighed. "See, if I were in your shoes, I'd have asked who requested them. No matter. To answer your painfully obvious inquiry, your services as a techno-mage are to be utilized. Effective now. I have your first orders."

From behind his back he produced a tablet Chris was far too familiar with.

"No way, forget it." Chris shot up on the defensive. "My days working for the Order are long over."

"I'm afraid not. Desertion isn't the same as dismissal. Technically, you're still one of us," Chase clarified. "And now that you're back, you'll continue your work. So, I suggest you clean up and review your mission. I'll send someone to fetch you in an hour."

Chase slid the tablet through the bars onto a nearby desk and left.

"Stupid redheaded psychopath," Chris muttered to himself once he could no longer see Chase. He stared at the tablet from a distance for several minutes before hoisting himself off the cot and over to the small desk. Picking the tablet up, he entered his old code. No surprise, the password still worked. The mission form was already pulled up and waiting for him to review.

"Fuck me..." he let out a breathless whisper when he realized what his orders were.

Chapter Three

The King of Dream Demons

"This is it. Nightmare's Gateway," Kit announced, hesitant. She'd led them to what Grady assumed to be the end of the Dream World. The journey hadn't taken them any time since the realm could be traveled in a flash for Kit, Ethan, and Mercury.

"Still want to go in with us?" Mercury tested Grady and Marcus.

"Go in *where*, exactly?" Grady did his best to try to hide the lump in his throat. The vast wasteland in front of them swirled with darkness. Before them an endless expanse of twisting, curling, smoky ebony vines contorted themselves into unnerving shapes. The only source of light in the cavernous dark of the land was the occasional lightning bolt that ushered whips of cold dead wind out toward them like a theatrical show meant to keep unwanted guests at bay. It had been quite a while since anything had given Grady goosebumps, but the hairs on his arms were standing at full attention.

"Nightmare's Gateway isn't so much a place as a state of mind." Mercury's scythe appeared in his grasp. They'd learned he only produced the blade when things were about to get messy. "All that's required of you is to suspend any disbelief you may have and cross the threshold. You'll find his home quite...immersive."

"Since you're most familiar with him, why don't you lead the way?" Marcus chimed in a dare. For once, Grady and Marcus were on the same page.

"As you death wish." Mercury gave a cheeky nod. He strode with confidence into the swirling oblivion. The smoky tendrils consumed him, and he vanished from sight.

"Will we even be able to survive going in there?" Grady asked Kit.

"I think so," Kit answered. "Depends on you, really. Just remember the truth. He'll try to make you forget what's real."

Grady frowned. "Well, that's unnervingly vague. Thank you, Kit."

She gave them an encouraging smile and bounded into the darkness alone.

"Second guessing your resolve?" Marcus teased him.

"Not at all," Grady defended. "Just trying to ascertain any helpful information before blindly jumping into what looks like a pit of cosmic despair. Yourself?"

"I'm a vampire, Hunter." Marcus smirked. "Darkness is my home."

He sauntered into Nightmare's Gateway without a second thought.

Ethan took Grady by the hand. "We'll go in together. I'll do everything I can to make sure we come back out together too."

Appreciating the solidarity, Grady squeezed his hand in return. They both allowed themselves to be engulfed by the Gateway.

*

They arrived in a clearing that reflected the Dream World, but Ethan noted the environment was its opposite in every way. Everything in this place was black and pulsing with deep-purple celestial energy.

Grady let go of Ethan's hand, collapsing to the ground beside a similarly unconscious Marcus.

"Grady!" Ethan knelt beside the two men and shook Grady's arm in hopes he would open his eyes.

"Let the record show I did warn them," Mercury said.

"Are they dead?" Ethan asked, horrified.

Mercury considered them. "No. Not yet, anyway. Look closer."

Ethan stared hard at them.

"Are you sure you were enrolled at a university?" Mercury sighed. "I mean with your powers. Use your powers to glean the truth."

Feeling stupid, Ethan followed instruction and placed his fingertips on Grady's temple.

"He's dreaming." Ethan released a relieved breath, knowing at least some hope of them surviving the trip existed.

"They're not Celestials like we are," Mercury explained. "They're prone to these sorts of psychic attacks."

"Attacks?" Ethan stood.

"This is Nightmare's doing," Kit confirmed. "He's testing them."

"Testing them for what?" Ethan's stomach knotted.

"Consider this a vetting process," Mercury said. "A home security system for the king of dream demons."

"Will they survive it?"

"That's up to them..."

*

Feldkirch, Vorarlberg
Austria
1858

The sun bore through Marcus's eyelids, and he woke in a flurry of panic. He tossed the sheets back and ran to pull the drapes of the window shut before any more awful daylight could attempt to devour him.

Once his labored breathing subsided, he realized he was back in his home in Austria. A place he'd abandoned several decades ago. Unnerved confusion set in, and a groggy mutter came from the bed. He whipped around to see Dacey laying naked beneath the sheets, the fabric trying its best to maintain some semblance of decorum by holding steady atop the one area that would verify he was entirely nude. Marcus noticed he, too, stood in the buff.

"What's happened?"

"What's happening?"

Their questions met each other in unison.

Dacey rubbed his eyes but made no effort to get up. In fact, he sank into the bed even more relaxed as though everything were completely normal.

"Where are we?" Marcus made no attempt to approach him. Instead, he scanned the room for possible answers and noticed everything remained just as it had been in his mortal life.

Dacey smirked as though Marcus was being silly. "In your chambers, love. After a night of revelry. Apparently quite too much for you. Are you all right? Massive headache? I see you've drawn the curtains. You know I love watching the sunlight dance across your skin when I wake."

"What on earth are you talking about?" Marcus's panic morphed into frustration. "Of course, I drew the curtains. We'd burn to ash otherwise."

Dacey blinked, his expression blank for a moment, and then he erupted into a fit of laughter.

"You really did overindulge last night!" His grin was scandalous. "You honestly believe we're vampires? And what's this nonsense about the Dream World and sandmen? Perhaps I should request a remedy be sent up."

"You can read my mind?" Dumbfounded, Marcus led himself back to the bed on shaky legs to sit as he attempted to process everything. Of course, he'd always known Dacey was telepathic, but Dacey had never been able to use his powers on him. Presumably because of his vampiric status. But if that were no longer the case...

Marcus bit the side of his own wrist and indeed drew blood. He was alive. He was human.

Dacey sat up in a flash now and yanked at Marcus's arm in what must have been an effort to save him from himself. "Darling, have you gone mad? You're scaring me. End this joke now."

"Everything you've said is serious?" Marcus needed full verification.

"I know it's uncharacteristic, but yes." Dacey kissed Marcus's palm to soothe him. "From now on, you're to stay away from opiates unless it's a modest tincture of laudanum."

Marcus had a hard time believing any of this to be reality. But the scenario must be. Dacey was real. He was real. And the more real the present situation all became, the more surreal all his memories seemed to become. Had his mind truly deceived him? Had none of those events ever happened at all? This was his true life. This was reality. His memories were becoming harder to retain.

His vampiric life had all been a dream. A nightmare. And that nightmare had finally ended.

"Perhaps a remedy would do me good." Marcus nodded, giving into the idea he'd slipped into a hallucinogenic state.

Dacey smiled as though that solved the problem entirely and climbed out of bed. "I'll send for one at once."

He pulled on his trousers and made a brief exit into the hall to inform a servant.

Marcus took a deep breath and rubbed his temples as hard as he could to force himself back into a semblance of composure. It didn't take long for him to put any thoughts of Mercury, vampires, and sandmen behind him. He'd much rather exist in this life where he and Dacey were lovers again. Even if he didn't really remember much of it. Dacey had come into his life after he'd been turned. At least, that's how things had happened in his nightmare. He couldn't remember how they met now. He could only hope the procured remedy would heal his mind and set things straight.

As Dacey returned, Marcus stood, trying his best to seem as though he'd gotten a grip on himself. He noticed his clothes laying on the floor and began to pull them on. That seemed the best place to start.

"Glad to see you're capable of greeting the day." Dacey smiled at him again, but this time his expression was less enthusiastic. He joined him in getting dressed. "You've got a big one ahead of you."

"I do?" Marcus faced him as he buttoned up his waistcoat.

Dacey replied, far too calm, "No need to belittle your moment on my account. I know my place."

Marcus picked up on his sour tone.

"Oh. And what is that?" He tied a knot in his cravat. Fishing for answers would be the easiest way to piece things together.

Or so he'd thought. Dacey stopped dressing and fixed an exasperated gaze on him. "Please, do not make me say it."

He seemed pained, which wasn't a normal Dacey disposition. They were both quite unlike themselves this morning.

Marcus raised his eyebrows in question.

Dacey shook his head and finished assembling his own attire, "I know you love me. And I know she's a fine prize. And I know we'll find a way to make this situation work. But please, don't taunt me. Not today."

"For fuck's sake." Marcus ripped his cravat loose despite having just secured the accessory. "What's so important about today?"

"Marcus"—Dacey again considered him with immense concern—"today is your wedding day."

Time propelled forward after the statement and Marcus stood before a congregation of family and prominent townspeople in lieu of the friends he'd never had. His bride-to-be made her way down the aisle toward him. He glanced over at Dacey, who had plastered on a smile to achieve the goal of convincing the world he approved of the union about to take place.

Marcus would've been surprised at his sudden teleportation into the event, but as he had already been in a suspicious state, the feeling just continued. He sensed something wrong about this entire scenario, and he couldn't believe the weirdness could all be blamed on any drug, no matter how potent the concoction may have been.

The fact was, he'd been here before. Never this far into the wedding, though, and certainly not with Dacey—who, during the previous time, he didn't even know existed.

His wedding day was one of infamy. He'd committed one of the most heinous slaughters of the century, murdering his entire family, several wedding guests that had arrived early, and his betrothed. Consequently, today was also the day he'd been sired into the world of vampires.

There had never actually been a wedding.

Yet, here he was, and now his bride stood before him. Petite with hair the color of raw honey and blue-green eyes, which sparkled as bright as the opulent jewelry she wore. Beautiful by all of society's standards but that didn't matter to him; nothing about her ever had. They were a boring match arranged for the same reason most marriages were arranged—money and status. The two things he disliked sharing most.

His mind wandered to Dacey again. The one glaring variable which stood out of place. He shouldn't be here.

"Stop!" Marcus shouted. "Stop! This cannot happen!"

The quartet, who were nearing the end of their song anyway now that the bride had taken her place, ended their tune a few notes early. All eyes opened wide with surprise, including those of his bride. Even Dacey, who cast a pleading stare his way as though Marcus were embarrassing them both. A few murmurs began to ripple through the congregation.

"Marcus! What are you doing?" his bride whispered in reprimand.

"This marriage is an illusion! A sham!" he shouted so all could hear.

The proclamation drew breaths of scandal and intrigue.

Dacey grabbed his arm and leaned toward him, "Darling, now is not the time—"

"He's right!" a voice boomed from the back. The bride's grandfather. He also happened to be the head of a prominent bank, one Marcus was set to be drawn into once the marriage was complete. He showed up with several lackeys following behind him. Marcus couldn't help but notice they were carrying ropes and mallets instead of more customary wedding gifts.

Marcus clenched his jaw. Now the setting was different even though this part remained unchanged. Apparently, this man could force him to see red no matter what timeline he existed in.

"I will not stand by and allow my granddaughter to marry a sodomite! We all know what a farce this union is!" the man spit, his words laced with venom. Now the congregation grew loud, shouting and whispering varying opinions.

The rest of the bride's family stood to face him.

"Enough of your nonsense! You're not welcome here with your vile gossip!" the bride's father pronounced. With equal disdain, he spun on his heel to face Marcus. "And you *will* marry my daughter! Whether you like it or not!"

"Everyone leave here now!" Marcus boomed in rage.

"If you want them married, there's only one way to fix things!" the old man countered at the bride's father. He waved his lackeys forward. "Remove temptation!"

The hate-fueled mob rushed down the aisle, shouting and knocking down guests who tried to stop them.

Dacey took off for the gardens attempting to make an escape. One of the men raised a pistol, firing the weapon in his direction.

Blinded with fury, Marcus's vampiric fangs returned. He dove into the crowd, and everything became a flurry of motion, blackouts, and screams. When the fray settled, he and the venue were drenched in blood, and no one was left standing. Not one of them. Frantic, he whipped around, searching for Dacey but found, despite his efforts, he'd lost him to the wound.

The taste of blood filled his mouth as he screamed at the sun, which did not harm him so instead the light might mock him.

When he woke from the rage, he was in Nightmare's realm.

*

The flickering flames danced a soothing waltz in the fireplace as the rain pelted down outside. Grady dozed off in a chair in his study as he tried to keep his attention trained on them. Their wild shapes began to lick against the surface of an object he spotted in the midst of the fire. Waking in full at the sight, he leaned forward in observation. It was a book.

Thunder rumbled in the distance as he squatted in front of the fireplace to get a better look. *The Mechanics of Sleep Travel*, the book's title read. Without hesitation he reached into the flames and pulled the book free. Miraculously, the tome remained untouched by any damage from the fire.

A loud clap of thunder shook the old manor, and the doors to the study flew open. Grady stood, clasping the book to his chest.

"Benny? Ethan? Is that you?"

No answer.

"Agatha?" he turned around with caution, knowing full well a ghost had no need to open a door to enter a room.

Again, no answer, but rain began to fall in the hallway.

"We have a leak!" He wasn't entirely sure what he expected anyone to do about the situation. He moved to the doors so he could inspect the ceiling. A black figure swept up the staircase on the other side of the pouring rain.

He gripped the book closer since he had every reason to believe they were an intruder. Their body had been too massive to be anyone else.

The book transformed itself into a pistol, and he stood at the foot of the stairs now.

He had a vague notion of how surreal everything happening to him was, but he was too consumed by the familiarity of the hunt. Alert, and with vigilance, he made his way up the stairs.

The hallway had become a dark shell of its former warmth as though the home had been abandoned for decades. The wallpaper had cracked, and everything lay covered in dust. Lightning illuminated the stretch enough for him to see Ethan's bedroom door was the only one open.

He cocked the pistol and ran to rescue him from the intruder, but when he entered the room, he reached the edge of the universe. Grady took a quick step backward to secure his footing. A few more inches and he would've been consumed by space. Yet there, floating in the cosmos before him, was a man of leviathan-sized proportions.

Humanoid but formed of the dream energy he'd seen from Ethan.

Grady could sense he wasn't looking at Ethan, however. The godlike sandman revealed two starfire orbs where his eyes should have been.

A voice whispered from the expanse, "Kill the monster."

For a moment, he was unsure which of them was being commanded.

The voice came again, sounding closer, and he knew it to be intended for him to hear. "He threatens the future of all mankind. Kill him and end this now."

Grady's heart slammed against his chest. He had no idea who or what asked this of him, but he knew the creature in front of him had to be the original Sandman. And there was no way he would kill Ethan's father.

"There's no other way," the voice prompted. "Kill the Sandman and stop Phantom for good."

"You're wrong!" Grady shouted into the expanse. The Sandman seemed eerily unaware of his presence and the conversation happening so near to him.

The pressure of the disembodied voice was unrelenting. "As long as the Sandman lives, so shall Phantom seek his crown. He craves the curse of Azoth."

Grady knew the terrible truth was the voice wasn't wrong. Eliminating either Sandman or Mercury would prevent the creation of immortality in its purest form. But doing so would mean killing Dacey, again. Or killing Vincent. He'd just seen his own father die as collateral damage in this cosmic vendetta. He'd be damned if he let his own role be in doing the same injustice to Ethan's father.

"Do it, Hunter."

"Do it yourself." Grady threw the pistol into the cosmos with resolve. He refused to be remembered in myth as the red right hand of whatever traitorous Celestial beckoned out to him.

"You would sacrifice all of mankind for this monster?"

"No," Grady stood firm. "But I will not kneel to the command of gods or exact murders they're too cowardly to commit themselves. And quite frankly, if things came to it, I would choose a future with Ethan over the future of mankind a thousand times."

The image of the Sandman disappeared, and Grady stared into an empty universe.

He wasn't alone though. The voice resounded, "Selfish mortal!"

"Perhaps." Grady crossed his arms in calm defiance. "And if that makes me just as much of a monster as you, then so be it. I'm used to letting people down."

The manor began to shake as a tremor hit, and the door frame cracked around him. He fell as the house lurched forward, tilting itself on one side. Grady struggled to grip the crumbling frame, but the piece of wood in his grasp broke off, and he fell without a sound into the cosmos.

*

"Welcome, creatures of the Night," the voice greeted them as Grady awoke.

On the ground, Grady choked and gasped as though breathing in oxygen for the first time. Ethan wrapped his arms around him in a tight hug, elated he was safe. He pulled him into a deep kiss; the fear of losing him having been far too real.

The kiss seemed to help bring Grady back to his senses. "What happened?"

"You trespassed," an unnerving, disembodied voice echoed around them.

Grady pushed himself back on his feet with the rest of them ready for confrontation.

"Yes, and now I'm sure they've learned their lesson and will never do it again," Mercury said.

"More than I can say for you...old friend." The voice sounded as if it were being sucked down a drain until it all emanated from one spot in front of them where the black grass shot up several feet in the same smokey black tendrils they'd seen outside. The smoke formed the shape of a terrifying almost-humanoid creature. Ethan thought the figure resembled a disproportionate, long-legged swamp creature. Its eyes were gigantic and glowed with the same purple starlight the rest of the world around them imbued. Despite the entity's terrifying voice, the creature did not seem to have an actual mouth to speak of—or from, for that matter.

Mercury smiled, a cunning grin Ethan hadn't seen from him since his days as Dacey the vampire.

"At one time, this land was a revolving door for me," Mercury acknowledged.

"And the universe will never be allowed to forget it," Nightmare reminded him in a callous tone.

Mercury's smile faltered.

Nightmare turned his attention on Ethan. "You definitely have a type, Mercury. It will be to your detriment."

"Actually, this is the son of my detriment," Mercury clarified.

"Aren't they all?" Nightmare countered. Ethan assumed he referred to every *somnium viator* who might have passed through the Dream World over the centuries.

"This one is a more direct descendant. Sandman is entrapped in his biological father's form," Mercury explained.

A loud clap of thunder boomed and then rolled through the realm around them. Everyone stepped closer to Ethan in protectiveness.

"Vincent," Nightmare stated.

"So...you already know?" Mercury prodded.

"I know your presence is a bad omen," Nightmare answered. "Why are you here?"

"I need your help," Ethan interjected, with a surge of bravery. He produced the orb and held it up so Nightmare could get a good look at the device. Another roll of thunder encircled them.

"How did you get that?" Nightmare demanded.

"Never mind that, dark heart. How does he use the orb without the Codex?" Mercury countered.

Nightmare fell silent for a moment, the starlight in his eyes burned bright as he scanned their group. Assessing in silence. Finally, he answered before turning to leave them, "*He* doesn't."

"He got the orb from me, and I didn't jump through hellfire hoops three times because of it for you to turn your back on us now. Give him the abridged lesson!" Marcus surprised everyone by shouting at the cosmic monster.

"*You!*" Swift as night itself, Nightmare returned in front of them to face down Marcus. "And who are *you*?"

"I'm Marcus von Rottal. Vampire. Murderer. Collector and dealer of esoteric antiquities. And quite frankly, the new thorn in your primeval ass if you don't give these men the assistance they request."

Nightmare's jaw unhinged into an unsettling abyss which began to suck away at whatever life force Marcus had within him. Energy swirled off Marcus's body with a rushing sound, like a vacuum, into Nightmare's mouth. He must not have liked the way he tasted because Nightmare clamped his jaw back in place and released him. Without breaking eye contact, he let out an intrigued breathy whisper, "Chaos bringer..."

Marcus appeared startled by the encounter but somewhat pleased with the title. Ethan had to give him credit. He held his ground well. With as much determination as before, Marcus again commanded, "Teach him how to use the orb."

Nightmare's attention now shifted onto Ethan as though reevaluating him in a new light. Ethan held the orb out once more.

This time Nightmare approached him. He lifted a giant sinewy hand and placed it on top of the orb as Ethan held the object from the bottom. The device activated, whirring back to action with its luminescent blue glow.

Faster than anyone could react, Nightmare punched his fist into Ethan's chest and clutched his heart. Ethan gasped, his entire body permeated with cosmic light, and his eyes rolled back in his head. He could hear Grady's shouts and someone struggling with him.

When Nightmare finally released him, Ethan took in a deep breath. His form returned to normal, but an unprecedented sensation of power surged through him. His vision cleared enough to see Grady had been held back by Mercury.

"Ethan, are you all right?" he asked with panic in his voice.

"Yes...I think so," Ethan answered, a bit shaky. At least he assumed he was all right, considering he was still conscious despite the fact the life had been sucked out of him for a brief moment.

"What did you do to him?" Grady demanded to know, still struggling against Mercury as though throwing a punch at a celestial being would do any of them any good.

"Transmutation," Nightmare answered. "Now he is reborn. Not Sandman but the rightful heir."

"What do you mean?" Grady snapped.

"He means Ethan is relinquished of his humanity," Mercury whispered to him with pity. "He is fully a dream creature now. Sandman's son, free to walk in his father's footsteps."

Mercury let Grady go now that the damage was done.

"What?! No!" Grady cried out. The transmutation had happened so fast there hadn't been a moment to stop it. He'd come all this way just to stand by and watch Ethan die after all.

Chapter Four

America's Most Hunted

The cool air nipped at their cheeks as Vivian and Thomas waited in awkward silence outside of a familiar building of horrors. Vivian had called upon her friend, Aubrey Blackwood. Well, she hoped he still considered her a friend. After leaving Marguerite's coven several years ago, she had managed to maintain good relations with most of them. That, however, became as severed as Marguerite herself upon the incidents of the past Halloween. She had received threats from a couple of members, others ignored her calls and apologies, so Aubrey—sweet soul that he was—appeared to be the only one interested in hearing her side and giving any sort of benefit of doubt. She hoped he'd believed her enough to agree to help her now.

Aubrey had worked for Marguerite at her occult shop and had informed Vivian that, after Marguerite's death, the coven decided it best for him to take over so the general public wouldn't go nosing about into the business of supernatural crimes. They'd simply say the former owner moved away, and he ran the business for her. Most people didn't ask too many questions. Most people aren't concerned with things which don't directly affect them.

The shop was usually closed on Mondays, but Aubrey had invited them over since he was there filling online orders anyway. Vivian only needed to ring the doorbell, but she hadn't managed to feel prepared enough yet. After all, the last time she set foot inside, this shop was under Marguerite's spell which caused her to attempt to sacrifice Ethan to a megalomaniac werewolf.

The cold weather must have made Thomas impatient because he felt the need to state the obvious, "Feeling like it's too soon to come back here?"

"Understatement of the year but what choice do I have?" Vivian sighed, gaining her composure. She pressed her finger to the doorbell. Thomas reached over and gave her a comforting rub on the back to let her know he supported her. Frankly, she was glad he'd chosen to come with her even if he wasn't happy about it. Thomas had been her rock through good times and bad and the past few months had proved nothing could shake his devotion; for that, she was willing to deal with the occasional overprotective complaint.

In mere moments, the door swung open and a beaming smile greeted them.

"Viv! ThomThom! It's so good to see you! How are you guys?" Aubrey gestured for them to come in out of the cold and gave them both welcoming hugs once they did.

"I won't lie, we've been better but it's good to see you too," Thomas answered. Aubrey happened to be her only supernatural friend, other than Benny, who Thomas liked. No surprise. Everyone liked Aubrey, and if they didn't, then he would make them; it was just his way.

"Come have a seat." Aubrey ushered them past the séance table to a patchwork couch Vivian didn't recognize. In fact, the shop seemed like a different place. Still a witchcraft parlor, no doubt, but everything had been moved around and updated. What once functioned as a den of dark magic now had the vibe of a sun-kissed boho hangout. She spotted a new counter in the corner.

"Is this...a bar?"

"Coffee and tea bar, actually." Aubrey beamed. As they sat down, he gestured to the coffee table in front of them where three cups sat already filled and steaming. "Help yourselves."

Thomas took him up on the offer.

"Marguerite never really cared about the business aspect of owning a shop. She just wanted a haven," Aubrey explained. "And while I'm guilty of utilizing the storefront in a similar manner, I also care about this place doing well. Adding in the bar has been a draw for college students keen on learning about the craft or just looking for a quiet and relaxing place to study. Sometimes people show up just to play Magic the Gathering." He flipped around a laptop for them to take a peek at, "Also, adding a website for online shopping has brought in a lot of business as well. This place is on an upswing."

Impressed, Vivian said, "I'm so proud of you Aubrey."

"I admit the circumstances were less than ideal," he said, addressing the elephant in the room. "But I believe in always trying to make the best of every situation."

"I'm glad that's your viewpoint because I hate to say we come bearing bad news," Thomas said.

"I had a feeling that might be the case." Aubrey grimaced. "It was in the cards," he explained and nodded toward the tarot spread laid out on the nearby table.

"I'll just get to the point then," Vivian said. "Grady and his partner, Ethan, are being hunted by some cult of alchemists—"

"Alchemists?" Aubrey raised a brow, his blue eyes shimmering with interest.

"Apparently. And they've kidnapped another man," she continued to explain. "We believe Grady, Ethan, and several others are safe for now but I'm sure they won't be for long. We need help finding these alchemists before they hurt anyone else and finding a way to contact our friends."

Aubrey pulled his legs up under himself on the couch and, brushing some long golden locks out of his face, leaned into the cushions. He steadied his gaze on her with amused incredulity.

"Let me get this straight," he said, putting careful emphasis on every word. "You want me to help you help the men you allowed to kill Marguerite? Why would I do that?"

Thomas jumped to her defense. "Marguerite put a spell on Vivian revoking her free will. She was killed by a monster *she* contacted in an attempt to enslave an innocent man."

"They say there are three sides to every story," Aubrey conceded after a moment of silent analysis. "Tell me more about this Ethan. What makes him America's Most Hunted?"

Vivian spent the next half hour recounting in full detail her knowledge and experience of Ethan and the situation they currently found themselves in. Aubrey gave her his full attention, his expression not giving away any judgment. His easy-going manner happened to be one of the things Vivian had always liked about him; it wasn't in his nature to pass judgment on others. He was usually very accepting. And, thankfully, wiser than his age and playful personality would have you believe.

"I'll do what I can to help," he offered, once she finished. He hopped up, rather eager, "Wait here just a moment."

"Two witches and a veterinary assistant," Thomas said as Aubrey disappeared into the storeroom of the shop. "Up against an unknown number of arcane magic users who clearly have more knowledge than we do. You really think this is a good idea?"

"No," Vivian admitted. "But it's the right thing to do. Besides, no one says we have to confront them. We just need to foil their plans."

"We're not living in a 1960s cartoon. They're not standing around somewhere twisting handlebar mustaches. These are real people, *bad* people, with a lot of power. They chased Grady away and as much as I don't like the guy, even I have to admit he doesn't back down from a fight easily. Maybe we should take that as a sign."

"I am. A sign *real* people need help," Vivian countered. "I thought you were on board."

"I am...reluctantly," Thomas reminded her.

"Then there's no point in discussing the matter further. We're doing this."

"But what is 'this'?" Thomas clarified his concern.

"'This' is this," Aubrey reappeared with a dusty book in hand.

"Why are the answers always in dusty books?" Thomas muttered. "You'd think if they had so much information, people would use them more often."

Aubrey returned to his perch and flipped the cracked leather-bound tome of gold-leaf pages to one that he had stuck a bookmark in to show them.

"No doubt this is where Marguerite found the rituals she needed to contact the wolf you described in the Dream World. There are all sorts of sleep and dream spells and rites contained in this grimoire. The one marked might do the trick."

Vivian took the book as he handed the tome over and scanned the pages as fast as she could. "This looks like a summoning spell."

"Mmm," Aubrey hummed in concurrence. "Similar to one, yes. Mixed with communion. You're opening up a mental pathway to the Dream World. It's like making a phone call and you must be very intent with who you're summoning or else anyone, or any*thing*, could answer."

Thomas rolled his eyes, "Great, a psychic pandora's box for witches. There shouldn't be any complications with that at all."

"This is exactly what we need." Vivian's optimism surged. "If I can speak to Ethan directly, then he can tell us how to help. This is a safer bet than anything."

"I don't think you know what the word 'safe' means," Thomas frowned.

"I agree with Vivian and as we're the only magic users in the room, your opinion kind of doesn't matter." Aubrey's bluntness hit hard.

Thomas scoffed. "Wow. Rude."

"What I mean is, we know our limitations and our strengths," Aubrey amended. "Together we can do this, and we shouldn't run into any problems. If your friend is in the Dream World, then it'll work like a charm."

"And what if he's not?" Thomas raised a brow.

"Then we turn to darker magic," Aubrey said as though the answer were obvious.

Chapter Five

More Than a Rescue Mission

"This is not what we agreed to!" Grady rounded on Mercury after Ethan's transmutation.

"You agreed to come here knowing risks were involved. This is precisely why I didn't want you tagging along." Mercury refused to make eye contact with him.

"I thought you wanted me to stay behind because you were concerned about my safety," Grady pointed out. They should've realized Mercury would be just as tricky as Dacey had been.

Mercury crossed his arms and flicked his wrist. "Well, that too. Naturally."

Nightmare let out a hollow growl that echoed around them and shut them all up.

"Open it," he commanded Ethan.

The orb unfolded its secrets with ease now; the vast starmap spread out around them.

"You are connected to his psychic frequency through lineage," Nightmare explained. "Ask him where he is."

"Where—"

"Not like that," Nightmare interrupted. He tapped his elongated finger between Ethan's eyes. "Like *this*."

Normally, Ethan would've been reluctant to believe something so simple could work, but he'd seen far too much to ever consider himself a skeptic again. Instead, he put all his energy into his own headspace and pleaded for his father to show him his location.

As he did, the map began to dart and twirl around them, making a fast trek through the cosmos.

Marcus ducked out of instinct as planets and stars hurdled by him even though they were just images, imprints fine-tuned by ancient magic.

The map halted, and a single planet glowed with a blazing blue fire.

"So, he does still exist." Nightmare scrutinized the pinpoint on the map. Ethan's heart raced at the prospect of finally meeting his father. "But how do I get there?"

"Dream," Nightmare answered. "String the stars together and create your own path. Now leave me be."

He began to dissipate into the murky shadows engulfing them.

"One more thing, old friend. When the time comes, will you help us defeat Phantom for good?" Mercury chimed in before he disappeared.

"Nothing is ever final, Mercury. All things are subject to change. You of all should know that. Either way, I will continue to exist," he said and vanished.

"Cheeky bugger," Mercury muttered. He threw his shoulders back as if it were no real matter and then turned to face Ethan. "I don't know who's more nervous for this reunion, but we might as well get on with it."

They looped their arms together to form a small united circle. Stricken by fear and elation, Ethan held the Orb firm in his grasp and dreamed them all nearly an eternity away.

*

"This is like training to be an astronaut," Grady groaned. Ethan tried to help Grady steady himself as he clutched his gut.

"Better get used to it," Marcus remarked, though in much the same position. "Otherwise, how will you ever survive your honeymoon?"

Grady couldn't help but chuckle, and Marcus smiled at him in a manner that might have been genuine.

Ethan, on the other hand, handled traveling just fine now that he didn't have human limitations holding him back; the process was already like second nature to him.

"Well, let's hope that worked because otherwise we're out of options," Mercury stated.

Seeing the barren terrain around them, Ethan, too, began to have his doubts. The only positive indication life may be supported here was the fact that the atmosphere seemed suitable since Grady was still with them.

"That thing doesn't happen to have a land-based GPS by any chance?" Grady joked, referring to the orb.

The orb had shut itself off and Ethan frowned a bit, wishing it did, as he pocketed the device. "I think we're on our own."

"Well, thankfully, I'm quite a good tracker," Marcus complimented himself. If there was one good thing about having a vampire along for the ride it was that they were able to whiff out signs of human life, and unlike Ethan, they knew Vincent still retained his humanity.

However, the air on the planet was hot, dry, and still. There wasn't much chance any scent here would carry at distance. They'd have to begin walking until they lucked into proximity.

As they traveled, they noted the planet itself was not much unlike a desert back on Earth. The glaring difference was in the sand which swirled a mixture of purple and white. If he weren't otherwise occupied with emotions already, Ethan would've stopped to take in its beauty. He made a promise to himself to return here someday with a proper means of mapping and documenting every new world he explored.

Not long ago, I thought I'd never do anything that mattered in life. Now here I am, poised to be the greatest explorer who ever lived. A funny realization. To be important in a way you never expected, nor planned for.

If he had to guess, half an hour had transpired before Mercury broke their uneasy silence. Ethan counted his blessings because he'd started to worry Mercury might be leading them on a wild goose chase.

"He's here," Mercury announced.

At the same time, Marcus must have picked up a scent because he also stated, "I've got him."

"He's not alone," Mercury added, sounding surprised by the fact. "Ready yourselves."

The warning came just in time since they were soon ambushed from behind the hills by a tall figure in some sort of muslin-style clothing and goggles and two teeny, but very fast-moving, alien creatures. The tall form could only have one possible identity and he didn't appear to be armed with any weapons, but the small aliens were, and they wasted no time in opening fire at Ethan's entourage.

Ethan went on the defensive and created a shield to block his friends from harm. When their strike hit the shield, Ethan could see they had only launched what appeared to be a netting apparatus, which fell limp to the ground as it missed its target.

The man jumped to the aid of his thwarted alien comrades, and with the same amount of ease that Ethan had created the shield, he ripped the barrier apart until the facade disappeared.

Ethan's eyes widened as the man caused Grady and Marcus to lose their footing and held them hovering in the air a few feet above ground.

Mercury, surely due to his own supernatural powers, was immune to the attack. The two wriggled mid-air, unsure what to do to break free.

Ethan thought about emulating the maneuver on the two aliens, but Mercury's wise words cut through, obviously having read his mind. "Play a better hand than that. Show him what you've become."

Ethan transformed with haste into his full sandman appearance, a Celestial body of pulsating dream energy.

"Let them go, Dad!" Ethan commanded.

The tall figure stopped in his tracks, releasing Grady and Marcus, who fell to the soft ground unharmed.

The man removed the goggles and wrapped mask from his face before crossing the short distance between them.

Once they stood only a few feet apart, Ethan morphed back into his human form. Vincent's eyes confirmed everything he already knew. After all this time, his father was still alive.

"Ethan," Vincent responded short on words. It wasn't a question. In fact, to Ethan, the statement felt like a welcoming home.

But before Ethan could be embraced into the loving arms of his father as he'd imagined this reunion would go, Vincent's attention darted to the two figures standing behind him.

"*You!*" Vincent growled. His eyes lit up with fury, and he bounded past Ethan to attack Marcus and Mercury.

Mercury teleported a safe distance from the impact, but Marcus was knocked square to the ground; a furious Vincent straddled him, gripping his shirt collar as he pinned him down.

For a moment, Marcus nearly struggled free, but Vincent sent a pulse of dream energy through his fists with the jolt of a defibrillator which would've been a shock if Marcus had still had a beating heart. Still, his anger seemed enough to dissuade the vampire from making another move.

"Tell me why I shouldn't kill you right now!"

Marcus glared at him as if daring him to try it but said nothing.

"Dad! Stop!" Ethan rushed to break things up. He grabbed Vincent by the shoulders and tried to pull him off. "He's my friend!"

Vincent froze, either because of the physical contact with his son or the statement he'd just revealed.

Marcus smirked. "Is that a good enough reason?"

Vincent settled for punching Marcus square in the nose before releasing him.

Marcus cried out, more likely in protest than actual pain.

Quick to his feet, Vincent didn't break eye contact with Marcus. "That *thing* is not your friend."

Without looking at Ethan, he pushed past him to rejoin his small alien cohorts who had been waiting to see what their next move should be. He signaled at them to depart back over the hill from where they'd first appeared. Ethan realized a moment too late he was leaving.

Bewildered, Ethan turned to Marcus. The vampire offered an annoyed sneer as he popped his broken nose back into place.

"I can explain," Mercury offered.

"Oh, you definitely will," Grady interjected. "But at this juncture, I feel it would be best if you two waited here."

He wrapped a supportive arm around Ethan's shoulder and prodded him to follow Vincent. Leaving Mercury and Marcus behind, they made their way over the small hill just in time to see Vincent slip into a small hut-like structure. They'd been right in his backyard, and they hadn't even realized it.

"I can't imagine this would've gone any better even if we had brought Arthur along. Go." Grady nudged him forward and found himself a place to rest on a nearby rock.

"You're not coming with me?"

"This sort of reunion doesn't call for a third wheel. I've nothing to say you can't say yourself."

"What about them?" Ethan shrugged in the direction of Mercury and Marcus. "You don't want to interrogate them?"

"I've had quite enough of those two to last several lifetimes. And I'm sure Vincent will provide a more honest explanation than they ever would." Grady gave another encouraging nod.

Ethan made his way to the hut and didn't bother knocking. He assumed Vincent had intended for him to follow. The unlocked door was validation enough. He stepped in, giving it a gentle snap shut with just enough force for a latch to click so Vincent would register his alien friends weren't the only ones with him now.

The entryway led to a modest dining area with little in the way of wares or decor. Ethan supposed there wasn't a whole lot which could be made with resources from a virtually barren planet.

Vincent stood across the room with his back to him. Silent but diligent, he grabbed strange tools and trinkets off a shelf and packed them into a tattered duffle bag.

Since Vincent didn't appear to intend on breaking the silence between them anytime soon, Ethan took it upon himself with the question that nagged at him when they had first made eye contact, "How did you know it was me?"

"You soul summoned me." Vincent continued packing.

"I what?"

Vincent seemed to attempt to slam the duffle bag shut, but the fabric top just fell in limp. He made up for it by yanking the zipper closed as aggressively as the bag would allow before he turned to face Ethan.

"That's how you found me, right? You projected your subconscious into the multiverse to link with mine," he said. "The only person with blood ties powerful enough to do that would be you. The last of us. And transmutated too."

For the first time, he fully took Ethan in. His gaze surveyed him, and Ethan relaxed since he didn't seem as angry as he sounded.

"I had help." Ethan pulled out the orb to show him.

The same hatred which had filled Vincent's eyes when he saw Marcus flickered back to life, and he rushed to take the orb from Ethan.

For a moment, Ethan thought he'd have to fight his own father, but Vincent grabbed the orb out of Ethan's hands and set the device on the table in disgust.

"That thing is a fucking menace," he said. "You don't need that."

Too grasped by emotion at being with his father again, Ethan couldn't even wonder what he meant. "I thought you were dead."

"Honestly, I thought I was too." Vincent gave no explanation for this statement either. Though, he did seem more sad than angry now. "I thought I'd never see you again."

Vincent embraced him in a tight hug, which Ethan would have let last a lifetime if he could.

Eventually, he managed to state the obvious. "I'm so glad I found you."

Vincent gave a small chuckle of amused elation. "Me too. Even if I don't like what the conditions seem to indicate."

Releasing him, Vincent mimed something at the small creatures who had been watching close from the corner of the room where they appeared to have their own lounging stations. They hopped up and ran to a small table where some handcrafted cups were stacked, filling them with a liquid Ethan could only hope was water. They delivered the two mugs to the table.

"Thanks, guys." Vincent took a drink.

They returned to their perches; this time, they were less interested in the conversation and more inclined to begin napping.

"What are they?" Ethan couldn't help but wonder.

"Friends," Vincent smiled. "Tuagani. I ran into them on a planet called Motusami. They witnessed one of my dream jumps and decided I must be a god or something. Never mind the fact I'd jumped above an ocean. You'd think a god would have better aim. To be fair, though, Motusami is eighty percent water. Anyway, the short story is they wanted less ocean in their lives, and I needed a good place to hide, so we traveled here together. It's good to have trustworthy companions if you can find them."

Vincent eyed Ethan with purpose.

"How do you know Marcus?" Ethan asked.

Vincent went silent. He studied the contents of his drink for a few awkward moments.

"Let's just say, whatever course of events led to your transmutation started long before you think they did. Did Marcus give you that?" He gave a small nod in the direction of the orb which now lay in the center of the table.

"Yes." Ethan answered, perplexed.

Vincent's jaw clenched. "How long has he been a part of your life?"

"Uh." Ethan had lost track of the days. "About a week."

That seemed to unruffle his father's feathers a bit.

"How is your mother?" Vincent changed the subject, and Ethan chose not to push the topic. He had gotten Vincent out of rage mode, and he hoped the truth would come out eventually.

"She's good," Ethan answered with caution. His mother's current situation was a bit more complex than he wanted to delve into. He wasn't about to tell his dad she'd fallen in love with someone else, and now she also had no clue if the second love of her life might also be dead. That would be more than awkward.

He settled for a half truth. "She's waiting for me in the Dream World. So is Arthur."

"What?" Startled, Vincent choked out an awkward laugh. "Okay. I had a hunch you sought me out for more than just a rescue."

Something about his tone made Ethan feel guilty.

"Start from the beginning, Ethan. How did these guys get you here?"

Confused, Ethan answered, "I brought them here."

"Because they wanted you to." Vincent seemed to pity him. "Give me the bigger picture, Ethan. What really led you to finding me?"

Chapter Six

A New Dawn Rises

Chase drew a small pocketknife from his suit and sliced the pad of his left index finger open. He placed the bloody digit on the prompt screen, which offered one of the few sources of light in the hidden hallway, and allowed the screen to scan his blood before beeping and allowing him passage. The magically guarded steel doorway then slid open, and he slipped inside.

He'd made the journey down the cold stone stairwell more times than any other living member of the Order, save for the man he was on his way to visit. These were the chambers of the High Alchemist, off limits to most, and where all their missions originated from. This was where contact was made. The chamber happened to be one of the most important rooms in the universe nobody knew about. As old as the man who had created it. Where the alter of Phantom was located. The lair of Verum Videns.

The Order's headquarters was a massive structure located parallel to the rest of the world—a magical haven constructed between veils and with the ability to open up anywhere on Earth that someone with the right credentials needed it to. The amount of arcane magic imbued into the structure's very foundation was awe inspiring and no doubt the reason the building had been able to stand for so long. If members of the Order were to believe its history, which they did, it was created by Verum Videns (Vid) ages ago. No one really knew how old Vid was or how he'd managed to circumvent Death for so long, and he wasn't the type to offer up any answers. He was not only one of the first alchemists the world had known, but judging from all he'd achieved in his lifetime, he had also been the most successful. In many ways, he was not really an alchemist by common standards; he'd kept the title because it suited enough as representation for what he'd spent his life trying to achieve. He wanted control over the most precious substance that existence had ever known. He wanted to be able to control and create Azoth: a quintessence of life-force, an energy created between Sandman and Death, that could make its host immortal.

That was the extent of the history of the Order most of its faithful members knew. But the few in the higher ranks knew the truth happened to be so much grander.

Chase had made his way to upper echelon of the Order in much the same way any man of power in the modern world had. Nepotism.

Although mostly human, Chase came from a rare and ancient bloodline. A son of Dawn. He'd never known his birth parents. As early as he could remember, he'd been under Vid's watch. Vid hadn't so much raised him as his own as he had trained him to be his predecessor if one were ever needed. According to the old alchemist, Chase's father had also been a son of Dawn but never wielded any power. Whatever gene carried Dawn's power must have been recessive when mixed with mortal DNA and waited to show up as soon as Chase was born—something they had to contend with until he'd unintentionally murdered them as soon as he could walk. Obviously, Chase had no memory of this, but considering the things he'd done in his life since then, he had no reason not to believe it.

None of this information had been told to him until his sixteenth birthday when Vid brought him into his chamber at the Order to show him what all his childhood training had been for.

That was the only time, until recent months, Chase had been allowed into this sacred space. Now, visits to the chamber were beginning to feel routine.

He reached the final steps of his descent and spoke the words necessary for what appeared as an empty dungeon to drop its illusion and reveal a grandiose sacred space filled with accouterments and an ornate throne with excessive detailing even King Louis XIV would envy.

He wondered if Vid had any notion that what Chase wanted more than anything was to set the world on fire. He'd sit in that very throne and watch the world burn around him. What a cozy night that would be.

"You summoned me."

Vid chuckled at his choice of words. "You may not be a demon, but you take just as much pleasure in a dramatic entrance."

"In a way, some people might argue that I am." Chase offered a self-important smile.

"Indeed, you are right." Vid left his alter where he'd been cleaning up some bloody ritual. He cut straight to the point. "You have a new directive."

He'd had the same directive since he'd learned the truth of why Vid had taken him under his wing, to capture and enlist the Sandman at all costs, so this caught him off-guard. He couldn't imagine anything being more important than that. For a moment he worried he might be being demoted for failing to apprehend him when he'd been so close.

"Well, a modified directive might be more apt." It was as though Vid read his thoughts.

Chase's shoulders relaxed, knowing his position in the Order was still secure.

"It appears our sandman is not the Sandman we thought him to be," Vid continued. "Only an heir. We were fooled. Vincent Roam lives, and Mercury is on his way with the others to find him."

"So, I don't need to waste my time with the scrawny dream weasel? Just re-enlist Vincent instead?"

"No, we still need the son. He can't be allowed to interfere with our plans," Vid said.

"So, what? You want me to kill him?"

"That won't be necessary. Just sedate him. Permanently. It never hurts to have a backup generator," Vid said. "And forget about re-enlisting Vincent. He won't be on our side any longer. Capture him. We're equipped to deal with him the old-fashioned way."

He was drawing on past precedent. In its beginning, the Order had captured sandmen before when their numbers were greater. They'd been sedated in the same manner he intended they sedate Ethan and hooked up to devices which allowed the Order to draw from their power, manufacturing temporary portals between worlds. A crude method they had little control over; without the discretion of the sandman to will them in a specific direction and without control of the Codex and orb, they had no way to choose where they might go. The Order had hoped they'd have the fortune of accidentally stumbling into the realm where Phantom had been banished, but that never transpired. They made use of the method regardless, spreading the Order through the multiverse and transporting various creatures from one place to the next to wreak havoc on worlds unprepared for the damage. This practice happened to be how Earth first came to have vampires, werewolves, and a few other of its supernatural creatures who easily preyed on humans.

Chase knew this method all too well. Vid had drilled their ways into him in case they ever had the opportunity to rebuild. The program had been active until the 1980s when it was destroyed in an uprising against Phantom by two former Hunters who had betrayed the Order under a demoness's command. All temporary portals disappeared, closing them off from the rest of the multiverse, and the sandman in their possession perished as well. The Order was left to pick up the pieces and refocus their efforts. The only optimism came in the form of a vampire who possibly housed the essence of Mercury. Thanks to him, Vid had obtained the Codex for a brief period. If only capturing Mercury was as easy as sedating a sandman, but to tap into Mercury's essence the host would have to meet Death and be allowed transmutation by Death's hand. Even then, Mercury could not be captured with ease; as a Celestial messenger, he was a strong telepath, which allowed him an advantage. For their plans to succeed, the Order would need to convince Mercury to choose to give himself to Sandman, causing Azoth to be created again. According to Vid, Phantom had always insisted this would be no problem once Sandman and Mercury were both reunited in their true forms.

For a brief time, Vid had been convinced he could force this reunion to occur in a somewhat organic way that wouldn't cause suspicion. He'd located Sandman and a vampire who might be Mercury. Vincent was easily swayed to work for the Order, but he'd had his suspicions since Vid later found he'd gone to some lengths to hide the fact he was married and had a child. When Vid sent the vampire to meet Vincent, hoping for the spark of destiny to ignite, he found himself swindled instead. Vincent went missing along with the Sandman artifacts.

Phantom had been furious. Twice now Vid had failed him. He had been instructed to keep close tabs on the would-be Mercury and the Order set out to try to find yet another sandman in a world which seemed to no longer have one. With no one else powerful enough to head the Order, Vid had been given a third and final chance.

Chase recognized his opportunity. The Order now had someone worthy of taking Vid's place; it's what he'd been raised to do. He only needed to procure both Sandman and Mercury himself, setting Phantom's will into motion, thus proving Vid useless. Chase would be the new High Alchemist of the Order of Azoth and, more important, the new ruler of the Earth. Rightfully. A son of Dawn in command of a kingdom which should have always been his. Not some bumbling geriatric alchemist with a proclivity for losing celestial beings.

"Not a problem," Chase accepted his modified challenge. "I'll find a way to get them here."

"No need. That's what I have the techno-mage working on." Vid smirked before turning away from him as if to quell his cockiness by letting him know he was still one step ahead of him.

*

Chris may have been free of his cell-like chamber, but he was more imprisoned than ever. The Order had branded him again, an archaic tradition of burning a locator spell into its members skin which would prevent them from ever trying to bail. He'd rid himself of the mark once before, but not only had the feat been the most painful process of his life, he'd also had to fake his own death to do it. A ruse the Order was now well privy to and would certainly not fall for again.

And his orders? To build a device which would interfere with the natural wavelengths of the universal subconscious, a mass dream disruptor.

Chris had no idea what happened to the others after he'd been apprehended by the Hunters of the Order of Azoth. He knew they'd escaped to the Dream World but that was all. Did the Order know where they'd gone? Was this a way to lure them back? Had Ethan already returned with Vincent as planned? Fuck all if Chris knew. The only thing he knew for sure was he'd be forced to work against them now until he could formulate an escape plan out of this mess.

He did his best to toil in the lab as long as possible, but he'd have to begin producing some results eventually. Otherwise, his existence was better stricken from the record in the eyes of the Order, and he'd be of no use in helping his friends when they returned if he were dead.

Chris took solace in the fact that as the world's best techno-mage, he was also one of the world's best illusionists.

Chapter Seven

The Sandmen

"I only ever wanted to protect you," Vincent said. He and Ethan sat together at the table inside his small dwelling.

Vincent had listened in earnest to Ethan's recounting of events. "I never trusted the Order. Not fully. I did everything in my power to keep my personal life separate from my work. Something never felt quite on the up-and-up with them. I knew if you ended up having the same abilities I did, they'd one day want to enlist you in the same way they had me. My intention was to shield you and your mother from that. I had no idea of the truth behind what they were really doing. At least not when I was working for them."

"But you found out?" Ethan had surmised as much when Vincent didn't seem surprised to hear about their celestial legacy. "So why would you leave? How could you protect me if you weren't even there?"

There was a flicker of rage again. Vincent glared at the orb for a moment.

"I didn't *leave*, Ethan. Someone tried to murder me by pushing me into a portal. I ended up in a strange world with no idea how to get back home."

"Why didn't you just go back to the Dream World? I'm sure Kit or Nightmare could have helped you."

Vincent's lips curled into a faint smile. "Kit's still around?"

"She's the one who helped wake my abilities," Ethan confirmed.

"Good girl." Vincent murmured to himself. He explained, "I had been pushed into the portal with a half demon who had every reason to want me just as dead as the asshole who sent me through. I don't know if I believe in destiny, or if because of our bloodline we're just prone to the stars aligning for us, but the portal I made to escape him led me to a kind of world I'd never seen before. Have you ever seen a ghost galaxy?"

"No..."

"Well, anyway. The name is a little misleading because the galaxy was very much alive. I had every intention of finding a way back to the Dream World but being stranded in a vibrant society, in another part of the universe, immediately sucked me in. I began to wonder about my purpose beyond everything else. I'd traveled to other places but none like that one. For the most part they were all uninhabited worlds similar to this one. I met a demon named Niccolo. He knew what I was as soon as he encountered me. He's the one who informed me of our history and what the Order had really been planning—"

"Wait," Ethan interrupted. "Who is he? How did he know all that stuff? Do you think he could help us?"

"He was no more than a historian, a keeper of knowledge. His insight was help enough." Vincent tried to squash any ideas Ethan might be percolating. "I learned the Order used to have transport bridges between worlds, powered by enslaved *somnium viators*. Luckily, they'd been destroyed before the Order found me because if I hadn't been so willing to participate in the Order's faux 'supernatural relocation program,' that probably would have been my fate too. Instead, the fake program was a way to use my gullible ass to explore new worlds."

"So, what kept you from returning to the Dream World?"

"The truth. I know who I am," Vincent revealed. "But I don't want to be him. If I go back there, then that's all I am, and that's what they want. He's all I've ever been to any of them. The Sandman. The lost King of Dreams. If I go back, then Sandman is returning, and I can't see a way where I wouldn't be giving the Order exactly what they've always been after. I know this isn't the answer you wanted. It's safer for everyone for me to stay hidden."

Dumbfounded by his father's resignation, Ethan asked, "So, you won't help us?"

"By staying hidden, I *am* helping."

"And what if you die? Then what?"

"If transmutation never occurs, then nothing. The Sandman no longer exists," Vincent explained with finality. He stood from the table and went to grab his bag from the counter as if to indicate their conversation was finished.

"You're martyring your life instead of fighting for it?"

"I'd be a martyr either way. I never had a choice." Vincent's voice became gruff and unwelcoming now. "I am glad you found me, Ethan. If only so that I know you grew up fine. Clearly, you did. Also, because now I can keep you safe like I've always meant to do."

"What is that supposed to mean?"

Vincent slung the bag onto his shoulder. "It means we're leaving. And we're not telling your 'friends.'"

"What? No way!" Ethan furrowed his brow. His long-sought reunion had turned into a complete catastrophe.

"No more hiding. You can't let Sandman die with you. I refuse to believe two Celestials with the power to create immortality through love should be forced into exile, or extinction, because some asshole with a god complex won't quit harassing them. I'm not backing down from this, and I won't let you either. With you, Mercury, and myself, all standing up to Phantom and the Order we should definitely stand a chance at defeating them for good. If we don't stand up to them, then no one will."

"Ethan, the Order exists for one reason. If we remove ourselves from the equation, then they have no purpose," Vincent insisted. "They'll cease to exist because we'll cease to exist."

"Will they?" Ethan challenged, "Or will they just start hunting down other Celestials with a new agenda? People hungry for power don't just stop, and we shouldn't cower to their terror just because we're afraid they *might* win. Phantom had been nothing more than a creature of shadows before he had Azoth, which he stole from Sandman and Mercury! We have to trust they can be stronger than him. I feel like...I feel like maybe even I can be stronger than him."

Vincent set his gaze on Ethan with surprise.

"And you think *they* really want to help you?" Vincent gestured outside back to where they'd left the others.

"They have so far," Ethan countered.

"You said Marcus gave you the orb," Vincent challenged. Ethan nodded, unsure of where he was going.

"Then I'm glad you found me for another reason," Vincent revealed. "I can save you from becoming bait. Tell me again who put the idea in your head about finding me? Because Marcus and Dacey are the ones who put me here"—he jabbed his index finger in the direction of the orb—"by tricking me into using *that* fucking thing. Marcus was the one who pushed me through the portal in an attempt to murder me. Dacey is Mercury, and now Marcus knows I'm the original Sandman and he's—what? Had a change of heart and wants to save me? Don't you see the trap, Ethan? There's no one we can trust but each other."

*

Mercury wasn't sure how long reunions should normally take. Time was a concept that hadn't meant much to him in quite a while. He knew he was being impatient, but he figured looming apocalyptic doom must surely be reason enough to feel antsy.

Without being in closer range, he couldn't read what was transpiring on the other side of the small dune, but his senses at least let him know they were still within walking distance. That much was a good sign.

Certain Vincent would expose the truth of his disappearance to Ethan, he wasn't thrilled at the prospect they could end up abandoning him out of distrust.

He glared at the back of Marcus's head, tempted to swat him like a misbehaved pet but restrained himself. There was a very real possibility Marcus would be the only one still on his side.

They waited in silence, seated on a rock, expecting the worst.

"What will happen to me when I die?"

The question hit Mercury by surprise, and he glanced over to see Marcus staring off at the alien horizon, introspective.

Mercury attempted to brush off the existential inquiry. "You're already dead." He'd learned long ago misplaced humor was the best way to let others know you felt very deeply about something but didn't feel comfortable opening up.

"When this form is taken from me, where will I go?" Marcus clearly wasn't going to back off. "What will become of me? You're Death, so you must know the answer."

"I do." Mercury paused.

His uncharacteristic reluctance to speak pulled Marcus's gaze away from the horizon and onto him, seeking further explanation.

Mercury offered his sympathy. "I hope you'll understand I cannot tell you. It breaks the rules."

Marcus modified his query. "Will I still be with you?"

"Yes," Mercury gave a careful answer and produced a smile meant to comfort him, but he could feel his own sorrow seeping through.

Marcus accepted the simplistic answer with a small nod and faced the horizon once more. "Then that is enough."

Relieved the conversation had ended, Mercury turned his attention back to the dune just in time to see another uncomfortable confrontation in store. Both Roam men were pulsating with starry-blue auras, and Ethan was in his pure sandman form. They were a storm of nightmares headed his way.

"Well, this is bound to be unpleasant." Mercury jumped to his feet, and Marcus moved to stand beside him.

Mercury intended to take them seriously but spotted Grady tripping over his own feet in the sand as he rushed to keep up behind them while calling something out. He couldn't help but laugh at the sight.

Mercury's amusement seemed to infuriate the Roam men even more as they approached.

"Did you think I wouldn't find out?!" Ethan glowed and not in the happy human way.

"Ethan, poppet. Your inner-monster is showing." Mercury tried to keep his voice calm and pleasant. Another way to indicate he found a conversation uncomfortable.

Apparently, that struck some chord with him, and he morphed back to his normal self, though still radiating a stardust aura like his father. Vincent stood firm beside his son, his eyes locked in a death glare with Marcus.

"The only monsters I see here are the two of you," Ethan accused.

At this juncture, Grady caught up with the rest of them. Clearly confused as to what was going on, he deferred to standing beside Ethan to observe and learn.

"So, you know the truth." Mercury locked eyes with Ethan and transferred the imagery of the fateful fight which sent his father through a portal and out of his life.

The experience disarmed Ethan, and his demeanor shifted. He was still angry but now only at one of them. He joined his father in his hateful glare at Marcus before responding, "I don't know if I'll ever really know the full truth. But I have decided something..."

He took a step back away from all of them. "Every person here has lied to me in some way, hidden things from me, and tried to decide things for me. Not anymore. I know almost as much as all of you, and I'm more powerful than some of you too. No one is telling me anything from now on. You're all going to start listening instead. Including you, Dad."

Vincent's eyes widened in surprise as he'd obviously assumed he would just be kicking ass not taking orders.

"We're not running away. No one is backing down," Ethan insisted. "What's going on is bigger than all of us and affects everyone. We're going to destroy the Order from the top. We're going to stop Phantom from ever being able to rule over anything. And we're going to do this together. No more guises, no more lies. Just a group of unworthy losers with one goal: to make sure the rest of the universe doesn't have to suffer just because we did. Got it?"

Proud, Mercury offered a slight bow. "I'm forever in your service. Both of yours."

He gazed into Vincent's eyes, knowing Sandman existed in there somewhere. Something must have clicked because Vincent's hateful expression subsided, and he stepped up to his son, resting a supportive hand on his shoulder.

"Count me in."

"I'd like to point out I have already been playing nice with people I hate for this mission," Marcus stated. "So, can we just get on with it, please?"

"Great." Ethan seemed relieved. "Just give me a second. Dad, I'm going back to get the Orb. Don't worry, it'll be fine."

He took off to fetch the device.

Grady, appearing perplexed as ever, chimed in. "I still don't know what has happened. Anyone care to enlighten me?"

Chapter Eight

The Son of Dawn

Chris hurried to put the last touches on the dream disruptor. The Order's plan was insane, or at least he guessed their scheme would be. They weren't the type to give a monologue on their evil plans within earshot, but it was a fair assumption anything they planned would be inherently crazy.

If they wanted to disrupt the dream frequency of the universe, that ultimately meant scrambling the universal subconscious. That sort of tampering would get Ethan's attention and the attention of any other creatures native to the Dream World. A disruption on a large scale of such a kind signaled war.

He hoped the Order wasn't counting on his ingenuity. The "last touches" he added to the device were his own illusion spells which would mask a hidden message, which he hoped would give Ethan an advantage.

That would be his special surprise for the Order. A gift for their welcoming him back into the ranks. Chris was a master at coding viruses. If he couldn't help in any other way, he'd be the Trojan.

He slipped the last masking spell over the small hexagonal device just as the door to his lab—or prison, as it were—slid open. Chase stepped inside, wearing a hooded golden robe with crimson lining.

"Rumpelstiltskin design that for you?" Chris hoped to catch him off guard so he wouldn't notice the last movement of his hands as he finalized his illusion. "On your way to the Met Gala?"

"I wonder if your friends found your incessant snark as obnoxious as I do." Chase diverted from his question. "I don't suppose you took the time while writing your next ill-performed stand-up routine to finish the device?"

"Heads up!" Chris warned as he moved to chuck the device in Chase's direction.

Chase's eyes flew wide open with concern as he moved to catch the device, only to realize a moment later Chris still had it in his grasp.

Chris laughed. "Sorry, I couldn't resist. Go low!"

He moved to toss the gadget underhanded, and Chase jumped forward, falling for the trick all over again.

Chris laughed even harder, still holding on to the device. "Man, how did you survive elementary school?"

"Enough!" Chase held out his hand, producing fire from his palm and threw the flames like a ball at Chris's head.

"What the—" Chris ducked, avoiding singeing his blue tipped hair by inches. He held up his hands in surrender. "Whoa-whoa-whoa! Okay, take it easy! You know what they say, all work and no play..."

Clearly still annoyed, Chase summoned a wall of fire and let the blaze loose on the lab table.

Surprised, Chris jumped back a safe distance. The remnants of his work went up in flames.

"I never play." Chase threatened through gritted teeth. He stormed forward and took the dream disruptor out of Chris' hands with force.

"You must have the tightest back muscles." Despite his joking, fear mounted inside him. He'd seen pyromancy before but never as powerful as this. The way Chase commanded the element was close to...godlike. *If he could throw out moves like that, why did he have the Hunters doing his dirty work?* Only one reason crossed his mind. Chase's powers were supposed to stay hidden. He'd just ticked off the Order's secret weapon.

Chase gripped the small device in his right hand and narrowed his eyes as he inspected the gadget with the utmost scrutiny.

Chris held his breath for a moment, hoping his masking spells were advanced enough to fool him. Thankfully, they seemed to work.

"You may be a pain in the ass, but your craftsmanship is divine." Chase slipped the disruptor into a silk pouch he produced from a pocket within his robes. "I'll try to refrain from killing you in case we need more assistance."

Chris frowned. "Thanks?"

"You're dismissed to your room for now." Chase turned to leave.

"I'm sorry, but I must have missed reading the back of your trading card." Chris stalled him, seizing the moment to glean what had to be valuable information. "Are you...human?"

Chase kept his back to him. "Of a higher pedigree."

"What do you mean?"

Chase was on the move again. "I mean while you were born of the soil, I was born of the sun." He paused as the door opened and he turned to Chris with a glimmer in his eyes. "Enjoy Earth's second twilight. Dawn will see that her son rises."

The door snapped shut behind him.

"Sunrises?" Chris murmured, racking the resources of his memory to try to decipher what the hell Chase could be talking about. There was something familiar in his threat, but Chris couldn't quite place it.

He jumped into the chair at the computer behind him, glad the electronics hadn't been destroyed in Chase's outburst. He had extremely restricted clearance, but there had to be some relevant information he could access somewhere, and he could break into just about anything; he was a techno-mage with a lofty hacker background after all.

The highest ranks of the Order were about to be distracted with the disruptor for a while; now would be his best chance to interfere with as many things as possible.

*

Chase knew he'd been careless. He shouldn't have responded to the traitor mage at all, but he was so close to the finish line that he got cocky.

The weight of the device bumping against his leg as he strode to Vid's temple served as a reminder that perhaps he shouldn't underestimate the techno-mage. Sometimes all it takes is one stubborn piece of dirt to stop the cogs of a finely crafted clock. After the ritual, he'd be sure to have Chris relocated to an isolation chamber where the Order's research team could get some practice on dissecting the brain of an advanced occult craftsman. Harnessing the essence of mechanical and analytical thought was bound to prove useful at some point in his reign.

But first, he had to see his plan through.

When he descended the staircase, he found Vid by no means alone. He hadn't expected him to be, but the sight of the rest of the council of High Alchemists was no less jarring.

Vid wore robes similar to Chase's, but the other three were converse, crimson lined with gold in contrast. Chase's chest puffed with pride and, admittedly, a bit of smugness. The difference in attire meant he outranked them. There was only one who stood in his way to the top.

"Join the circle, brother." Vid invited him into their ranks, his voice stoic.

As he took his place in their circle, he made it a point to make eye contact with each of the others, so he knew their faces and to ensure they knew his. None of them were human. One was a Shadow Man, the race who retreated to the darkened corners of the world after Phantom's exile and appeared to exist only to observe.

The next, with her slender frame and angular pointed features, was of the Fae. *So, they really do exist.* He'd never seen one before, and now couldn't imagine why they hid their true forms. She was magnificent. He promised himself once he began the world anew, all superior creatures would finally be comfortable to come out of hiding.

The final member of the council was the one Chase had first spotted upon arrival. He couldn't be missed. He didn't wear the hood of his robe up due to the simple fact that he couldn't. The giant antlers protruding from his head prevented proper cloaking and caused him loom over the rest. His beady black eyes shimmered with eternal dark wisdom. He had tawny-brown fur laced with grey. He was, as much as Chase could determine, some sort of jackalope. *I thought bunnies were supposed to be cute.* This creature was the extreme opposite of that stereotype. He twitched his nose in Chase's direction, apparently judging his scent.

Chase recoiled in the jackalope's presence, especially once he noticed the froth around the monstrous rabbit's mouth. Chase diverted his gaze to Vid, pretending his full attention to their leader came from deference, not because he'd just imagined a large bunnyman ripping off his face with its ancient yellowed fangs.

Taking this as a sign he was ready to begin, Vid held out a palm to the stone slab that made the center of their circle. Chase retrieved the disruptor from his robes and set the device on the altar.

"The son of Dawn will now offer his blood in trade for our passage to the subconscious realm." Vid wasn't informing any of them of what they didn't already know; he was invoking the ritual.

Chase drew the athame, which sat alongside the disruptor on the altar with a few other items. He slit his palm and allowed his sacred blood to trickle free, with purpose, into the chalice next to him. The cup was as old as everything and everyone else here. He wondered how many rituals the chalice had seen and whose blood it had contained over time.

When he finished, the Fae woman approached to take his hand, healing the cut in an instant. As she gazed into his eyes, a spark of unity ignited. The Fae were truly an embodiment of Earth's natural magic and beauty. He'd never understand how Dawn had allowed humans to claim dominion over Earth when there were beings so much more worthy of ruling.

They rejoined their places in the circle. Vid's invocation sounded like cosmic poetry, and in moments, the device hummed to life, transmitting into the vast eternal planes of the Dream World.

Chapter Nine

Disruption

Trust levels worse for wear, Ethan still managed—with Vincent's help—to get everyone back to the Dream World safe. He made the conscious effort to not have them all just pop right back into Kit's den. He knew the reunion with his father would be shocking enough for his mother. No need to have him figuratively, as well as literally, showing up out of thin air.

He surely had a hundred more important things he needed to be thinking about at the moment, but a huge part of him couldn't help but toy with the wonder of what this would mean for them if they survived—*when* they survived—defeating Phantom. It's not as though they would just instantly become a family again. Too many years, and Chris, stood in the way of that. If Chris was still alive. A pang of worry hit Ethan, knowing how short on time they were. Hopefully, Chris would still be out there somewhere waiting for them. As excited as he was to bring his father back, he had grown to like Chris, and Chris had put his life on the line to save him. He wasn't even sure at this point which man was more deserving of his mother's love. The choice would be hers alone to make, one he didn't envy, but he'd support her decision no matter what.

All these thoughts happened in the instant of transport, and now they were all firmly in the Dream World.

Mercury had taken Vincent to the side attempting to smooth any ruffled feathers and, Ethan suspected, to see if he could get through to Sandman. He assumed Mercury's priority, at this point, would be convincing Vincent to embrace his origins and become the Sandman again. Validity of this assumption was supported by Marcus sulking near a tree, pretending to rest but unable to mask his occasional glares in their direction.

Ethan let out a heavy sigh at the cosmic melodrama his life had become. Just months ago, his focus had been preparing for piano recitals and thinking his nightmares were nothing more than signs of a chemical imbalance. They say adulthood changes you. Whoever *they* were, they had no idea.

"You're handling this magnificently." Grady's accented whisper filled Ethan with warmth and a welcome sense of stability. He turned away from the theatrics of the others and produced an amused, but tortured, smile for Grady.

"It's a mess." He choked out a small laugh.

Grady shrugged. "Things could be worse."

"I honestly don't know how they can be."

"Things can always be worse. It's the one constant in life. The universe gives us just enough slack to remember we can strive to make things better."

"Where do you get this stuff?" Ethan grinned despite their dire situation. "You're like my personal Jiminy Cricket."

"I'll take that. At least the little bugger knew how to dress." Grady smiled, causing his crow's feet to show. Ethan loved them, each and every earned line.

"Well, I'm glad you think I can handle this because every ounce of me wishes one of my abilities happened to be time travel so I could go back to being in your bed and happily ignorant about all of this Phantom, Sandman, save-the-world bullshit. I just wanted to play a piano and have hot sex with my British boyfriend every day for the rest of my life. Too much to ask for, I guess."

"If it makes you feel better, technically you don't have to save the world. Your father does," Grady encouraged. Cheekily, he raised an eyebrow. "Every day? For the rest of your life? Do you really..." He trailed off into some thought Ethan could only wish he knew. Sometimes he envied Mercury's telepathy.

Ethan wanted to offer the same encouragement, so he answered with a simple but pointed, "I do."

He thought maybe Grady would laugh or make another flirtatious comment, but instead, his eyes weighted with tears, and he shifted his gaze to the ground, consumed with introspection.

Ethan knew reality couldn't be dispelled by wishes and obstinance. The universe wouldn't let him *just be*. He'd have to see things through to the end, and then, maybe if he was lucky, something would go his way.

"You're not human anymore." Grady's simple statement of the truth seemed to come out of nowhere and pierced Ethan in ways he'd never imagined. Was that what Grady thought? That they couldn't be together anymore? That Ethan wouldn't still want him?

Before he could respond with his unconditional love, a high-pitched static broke through the aether of the Dream World and grated against Ethan's senses like the brakes of a speeding train grinding to a stop on a cold steel track. Ethan saw Vincent clasp his hands over his ears too at the sound, but the noise overwhelmed Ethan.

He fell to his knees, overwhelmed by the din and life's relentless bullshit.

*

As the one with the closest connection to Ethan, Vivian chose to be the conduit for their spell, which didn't surprise Thomas but made him even more anxious. They had formed a simple three-person circle on a vintage rug, and Aubrey spoke the incantation while Thomas did his best to stay open minded and positive as he'd been instructed. He wasn't a skeptic by any means. He'd seen enough during his relationship with Vivian to know witchcraft was indeed real, but he'd also seen firsthand how easily magic could go wrong. He'd have to put all these worries aside while the spell was performed in order not to pique the interest of any darker spirits who might be lurking around the aether waiting for a weak mind to allow them passage in.

As much as he fought Vivian's friendship with Grady—in fact, the reason he did, was he loved her being a witch and was always very proud and impressed by her— he just hated the idea others would take advantage of her power. He'd maintained the belief Grady had only used her to his advantage—another tool in his box of self-serving supernatural weapons. Thomas wished she wouldn't put her own safety on the line so often for someone he didn't agree deserved her protection. Someone he wasn't sure would do the same for her. That night when everything had gone wrong, Grady wasn't focused on saving Vivian. Thomas had saved her all by himself. Yet here she was again, putting herself in danger to make sure Grady was all right. As soon as they knew he was safe, Thomas would probably punch him.

Something in the atmosphere around them changed, and he assumed that meant their magic was taking effect.

He did his best to wash his mind of all thoughts other than the summoning spell Aubrey recited.

He could've sworn he'd fallen asleep, but he had enough wherewithal to know he was still conscious. Vivid imagery blurred around in his mind, out of sync with the disembodied voices they should match. There were fragments of a scene which reminded him of static interrupting a television signal. For a moment, he swore Ethan was on his knees beside someone, and his hands were covering his ears as though shielding himself from an explosive noise. The static swept the image away, and a terrifying creature began to climb out of the shadows. The nightmarish monster opened its jaws wide to reveal a pit of absolute darkness. The creature emitted a guttural noise which sounded like the word, *"Phantom"*.

Thomas considered shouting that they should stop the ritual, but thankfully, the frightening monster succumbed to the overpowering static and faded away. The scene morphed back to Ethan who stood again with Grady and a few others who Thomas didn't recognize, except Dacey.

Vivian's voice broke through, and recognition crossed Ethan's face.

"I'm here to help, Ethan. Tell me what to do," she implored. His eyes widened with surprise, but before he could answer, static interrupted them again.

This time the disruption did not recede. After a long stretch waiting for a sign— they were still connected— something else came through loud and clear. A man's voice, which broke in midsentence.

"—*if* you hear this. Please tell Karen I love her. She already knows, but I just needed to put that out into the universe before I die because she's the only good thing that ever happened to me... I repeat, Ethan, the Order is using a disruptor to try to weaken the integrity of the Dream World. They're smoking you out. They want to bring the fight to Earth where they know they have an advantage. I'll try to destroy the disruptor, but there's a chance I won't be around for long after this message gets out. The disruptor will prevent your powers from working properly, so it must be destroyed. Once it is, coax them onto your turf. Their headquarters are located adjacent to Earth's dimensional plane. The celestial coordinates are encoded in this message. I don't have much time, so when you hear this, *if* you hear this, please tell Karen I love her. She already—"

The message played on a loop until Ethan's voice broke through the noise and gave them their instruction, "Vivian, follow the coordinates and save Chris!"

*

In an instant, the spell broke. Thomas was back to his full conscious state along with Vivian and Aubrey.

"What the hell?" Thomas took a deep breath to center himself, and he turned to Aubrey for an answer.

"Not quite what I'd imagined would happen, but still effective," Aubrey stated proudly before she snapped the book shut.

"How am I supposed to travel to a parallel dimension on my own?" Vivian looked overwhelmed. "I don't even know what this Chris guy looks like. How am I supposed to save him?"

"It sounds like Ethan listens to others about as well as Grady does. The guy said we need to destroy that disruptor thing, not go on a rescue mission," Thomas interjected. He could tell by her expression she wasn't going to listen either. He sighed. "At least you know now they're alive."

For once, she seemed relieved. "Yes, thank the Goddess."

Aubrey must have sensed the tension. He stood and headed toward the front desk of the shop. "I'm going to see if someone I know can help."

At this point, a private conversation seemed unnecessary. Thomas had nothing else to say. They were putting their lives on the line, and if Vivian thought the most important thing was to save Chris, fine. But while she did, he would focus on finding the disruptor.

*

"Did it work?" the Fae woman asked Vid, the question Chase wondered as well, as they broke their ritual circle. The Shadow Man must have had more confidence because he receded to a shadowy chamber exit, unconcerned with hearing the answer. Chase wondered what strange corners of the world he called home.

The device still hummed its magic on the slab.

Vid took her hand in a friendly farewell. "It appears so. Time will tell. We have all of our eyes watching around the world for any sign of his return."

She offered a graceful bow to him and then turned to face Chase. "It's an honor to meet you, Chase. Vid speaks of you often."

"The pleasure is entirely mine." He too took her hand and kissed the back of it, offering up his most charming smile. "And what is your name? Vid's tongue hasn't been as loose with me."

She smirked and turned to Vid. "This one is trouble, old man," she said with a rich mesmerizing accent Chase couldn't place.

Vid chuckled as though he could possibly have any idea. "He keeps things in motion. That much is certain."

"An Elemental's purpose. I would know." She turned back to Chase with a forgiving smile. "As would any son or daughter of Dawn. My name is Lauma, brother."

All the warmth drained from his face. Chase's unprecedented expression of shock must have been amusing because both Lauma and Vid laughed.

She said her goodbyes and took her leave.

"Elemental?" was all Chase could manage to spit out as he tried to salvage his dignity.

"I may have forgotten to mention that part. The High Circle of Azoth is formed by Earth's most powerful Elementals, yourself included. You command fire. She commands air." Vid seemed far too pleased with himself at having kept such a damning secret from him. Chase wasn't the only living child of Dawn after all. "Nu, the abyss, is of the water. Tuft Stuff is of the earth. You are all four the heirs of Dawn."

"His name is Tuft Stuff?" Chase eyed the giant jackalope with curiosity as the animal proceeded to scratch behind its ear with its hind leg, utterly disinterested in their conversation.

Vid shrugged. "It was between that and Beast Bun. He preferred the former."

"Why did you never tell me I had siblings?" The warmth returned to Chase but this time the heat was drawn from his ire.

"Because I know you're trouble. You've always had a temper and I watched you grow into a vindictive and narcissistic murderer."

"You raised me that way," Chase reminded him with a glower.

Vid cast a calm stare at the disruptor with his hands held behind his back. "There is always one bad seed in every family. Multiples the richer the bloodlines get. If I had told you in the past you had siblings equally as poised to be the heirs of Dawn you would've dedicated all your time and focus on removing the competition. We would not have been able to achieve what we did today, and the Order always takes precedence. I've had to always keep you two steps behind for the good of Phantom's cause. At least long enough for you to learn your place and keep in line."

"And now that I have, am I still two steps behind?"

Vid's silence was all the affirmation he needed.

"You can't keep me in the dark forever," Chase threatened, throwing a fireball at him. Vid transported himself away with a shadow-walk spell, leaving before he took the heat of Chase's wrath.

"Coward!" Chase shouted as though there were some way the old alchemist would still hear him. But he knew he'd probably be in his private quarters by now.

Chase turned to the jackalope. "Leave before I turn you into dinner!"

He flared up another fireball.

Tuft Stuff let out an angry low honk of a squeak but hopped away into the shadows, disappearing just as Vid had.

Chase glared at the disruptor, still working its magic alone on the altar.

"I'll burn every last one of you until the world is illuminated." He threw the fireball at a dark corner of the chamber. "Shadows will cease to exist, and I will never be in the dark again," he vowed to no one and everyone all at once.

Chapter Ten

Traps Set in Motion

"I can't believe they found us." Grady grinned in response to Chris's and Vivian's cleverness after Ethan relayed the mental messages he'd just received. "I'm not so bad at choosing friends, after all."

"See, she didn't abandon you. Just needed some space." Ethan offered a reassuring smile which faltered upon the grim expression clouding Vincent's features as he rejoined them. It was easy to guess what had caused his upset.

"You...failed to mention Karen has a boyfriend."

"Yeah..." Ethan couldn't hide the guilt creeping into his voice. He supposed it was unfair to try to send his father in for a reunion without a proper relationship status update. But after hearing Chris profess his love, Ethan realized his selfishness.

Thankfully, his father seemed to assume he'd withheld information for a different reason. "I still would have helped you. You're my son."

"Yeah." Ethan nodded, glad at the reprieve from an explanation. "Yeah, of course. I know." He shrugged as if to say, *Silly me. What was I thinking?*

Vincent cleared his throat. "I don't think now is the best time to see her. Which sounds insane to say out loud considering how long I've wanted nothing more than that." He gave a tiny pained laugh.

Mercury and Marcus had rejoined them by this point, always game for gossip.

"Well, there's more than enough to keep you busy." Mercury, privy to Chris's message by way of telepathic eavesdropping, got right to the point. "One of you needs to pay a visit to our friends at the Order, and Ethan isn't exactly Magellan when it comes to following coordinates."

"What?" Ethan was less offended by the slight than by the idea of sending the Sandman right into their stronghold. "No way! He can't go there."

"He can and he should," Mercury replied with finality.

"He's right." Vincent surprised them all by agreeing. "They'll be expecting you. Not me. And I know how they operate."

"But what if they capture you? You're the one they're really after," Ethan reminded him.

"I'll make sure they don't," Marcus interjected.

"That will be hard considering you won't be there," Vincent stated in a tone clearly meant to warn him he should backtrack on whatever he was planning.

"You can blip around all you'd like and throw sand in their eyes or whatever it is you creatures do but when it comes to stealing highly guarded magical objects, you'd be remiss not to utilize my expertise."

"The only time I've been on a mission with you, you tried to kill me." Vincent glared.

Marcus shrugged the accusation off. "People can change, you know."

"I must say, the thought of the two of you having to work side by side both terrifies and arouses me," Mercury admitted. "While I can see a number of drastic ways this could go sideways, I have to agree it's probably our best chance."

"You expect me to trust him?" Vincent refused to even glance in Marcus's direction.

"No. I expect you to help him," Mercury ordered. "If anyone can steal and destroy that thing, it's Marcus. All you have to do is transport him in and back out again in one piece."

"And what about bringing them to fight us here?" Ethan reminded them. "How do we plan on doing that?"

"It's time you stole a few tricks out of Sandy's old book, Ethan." Mercury's lips turned up in a devilish smile before addressing the others. "You two, go," he ordered Vincent and Marcus. "Grady, inform the others of what's to come and protect them if need be. Ethan and I will handle leveling the playing field."

"You had better know what you're doing," Grady warned him.

"Don't I always?"

He answered with a confident, "No."

Grady squeezed Ethan's hands to show support anyway and gave him a kiss for good luck before taking off to do his part.

Reluctant, Ethan pulled out the Orb and tossed the device to his father. "Be careful."

To Marcus, he cautioned, "Don't make me have to find him again."

Marcus rolled his eyes.

"I'll be fine." Vincent tried to reassure him. "I love you, son."

"I love you too, Dad." Ethan offered a heartfelt smile.

Vincent brought the orb to life and entered the coordinates. He took Marcus's hand with a side-glance of mistrust, and in moments they were gone.

Ethan turned to Mercury, "So, what tricks have you got up your sleeve this time?"

"Think of them more as family secrets," Mercury answered, coy. "Let's pay another visit to Nightmare, shall we?"

*

Chris slumped back in the computer chair. His mind whirled with the implications of what he'd discovered. The fact that Chase had been so bold to say the fact to his face, even though it took some research to discern what he meant, was proof enough they were in over their heads.

The son of Dawn. As in the Celestial Dawn. *Damn.*

Not only that, but Dawn was quite the prolific Celestial. There were several children of Dawn, Elementals, currently living, and all of them had ties in some way or another to the Order. This was problematic. Power was power, and in the end, as far as he knew, the only Celestials they had on their side were Ethan and Mercury. They were severely outnumbered and most certainly uninformed.

The magnitude of their predicament weighed on him. They were swept up in a centuries old battle with the forces who had essentially created the reality they all lived in. Outnumbered and uninformed was an understatement.

He had no idea if his transmission spell had worked. He hoped Ethan had got the message. Until he heard any indication of infiltration or the destruction of the disruptor, he'd have to assume he was still the only one working from the inside to try to put a stop to them. He'd have to try to get the disruptor back himself, but after witnessing what he was up against with Chase, he had work to do to prepare for such an endeavor.

Chris hopped up and began to gather pieces from all around the lab, breaking a few instruments, if necessary, to obtain parts.

He'd have to fight fire with fire. Or, at least, with firewalls.

Chapter Eleven

The Swamp Wizard

What seemed like the longest hour in history to Vivian eventually resulted in Aubrey finding someone who could help them break the veil between dimensions.

"One of the great things about living in a small town is when you're searching for buried secrets there's not as much terrain to navigate," Aubrey had said before they left the shop.

Still, Vivian couldn't believe it had been so easy; she knew so much about the supernatural side of Shady Pines but there were still so many secrets her acquaintances were hiding. Thankfully, Aubrey had a personality which could get on everyone's good side enough they'd confide their knowledge and abilities without care. He didn't even need to use magic. The power of an active listener with a genuine smile.

They were now well on their way, driving to the outskirts of town to the marshes.

"I feel like we should be listening to Lou Rawls. Or Rob Zombie," Thomas said as the road they were on changed from asphalt to dirt. The loblolly pines gave the illusion they were encroaching around the vehicle of their own accord as they became denser and denser.

Thomas turned his high beams on to make sure he didn't hit any wildlife as he drove them further into the marsh. "I mean, what kind of person lives in a swamp of their own volition?"

"To be fair, he's lived there for over a hundred years," Aubrey pointed out from the back seat.

"If that's meant to be comforting, it's not," Thomas said before falling into an anxious silence.

Vivian wasn't nervous in the slightest about who they were going to meet. She'd met him before but had written him off as a pretentious old warlock who preferred a shamanic lifestyle because he assumed living such a way gave him more credibility. Dacey had once told her he found the man to be a complete bore, and she trusted Dacey's intuition when it came to people and social situations. He did have the ability to read their minds, after all. Apparently, wielding arcane magical knowledge must not have been very interesting to the vampire because it turned out Rhun happened to be more powerful than anyone had given him credit for. If she had the ability to do what he'd told Aubrey he could do, then she'd probably be pretentious too.

After a tense drive, Thomas parked the car by a small clearing beside an old wooden shack on the edge of the water.

"Oh yeah, I can see the appeal... If you were Jason Voorhees." Thomas stared at the rundown house for a moment with complete apprehension.

"You might want to save your nerves because this is the easy part," Vivian advised. To try to put his mind at ease, she leaned over and gave him a supportive kiss on the cheek.

The backseat door shut. Aubrey was already on his way to the shack.

Without further reluctance, Thomas followed suit. Vivian got out and joined Aubrey, who had already knocked on the old wooden door.

When the door flew open, they were met with the scent of rotting wood, slight body odor, and fried chicken. Rhun, in ritual robes, ushered them inside.

"Is that KFC?" Thomas asked. The bucket of food was set out on a small table in a combined dining room and kitchen. There wasn't much of a living room to speak of. Just an old fabric recliner which had been pushed up near a wall to face a small television.

"Indeed! Love the stuff. No one likes performing magic on an empty stomach." Rhun offered a welcoming smile as he led him over to the table. "Feel free to help yourselves."

Vivian wondered how he'd managed to get the food so fast but shrugged the thought off. There were much more important things to talk about.

"Thank you but we'd like to get down to the grit of things," Vivian interjected as soon as Aubrey hovered hungrily over the food. Keeping men on track proved to be as difficult as wrangling werecats.

"Ah, yes. Eager to pierce the veil." Rhun gave an empathetic smile. "I must admit, it's been quite some time since I've had guests with such a lofty request."

"I apologize if we're being too forward, but our friends are in danger."

"It's been my experience most friends wind up in danger and the reason why I try not to keep too many," Rhun said.

Vivian had a feeling he was only half joking.

"Don't worry one bit," he added. "I'm glad to help. I've been needing to stretch my magical muscle. You never want to let yourself get too rusty. They can sense weakness, and I can't have them taking this place back. The land itself is filled with too much power."

"They?" Thomas rested his arms on the back of a chair and leaned forward a bit with interest. He was obviously not comfortable enough to sit down.

"The will-o'-wisps," Rhun answered frankly, taking a final slurp of the soda which had been in his hand. He gestured with the cup as he spoke. "This place was given to me by an old friend. It's imbued with kelpie magic and sits on a ley line, which is part of the reason why I asked you to travel out here in order to help you out. Believe me, as soon as I die, those things will tear this place apart. They're not exactly fans of humans who wield borrowed power."

"Borrowed power?" Thomas's brow furrowed.

"Sounds like you need to take a class or two, kid." Rhun smirked. "I don't have time to explain everything. I think Aubrey still teaches Ethical Use of Magic on the weekends."

Aubrey nodded to Thomas. "We have a Facebook group you can join if you're interested."

Thomas squinted his eyes and shook his head.

Rhun set down his empty cup and clapped his hands together. "Well, let's get started, shall we?" He propped open a side door which lead straight to the swampy water.

"Have you heard of the Order before?" Vivian asked as she joined Rhun's side.

"No, I can't say I have." Rhun walked them right to the edge of the boggy water. "Then again, I don't get out much anymore. But if they're as powerful and as terrible as they sound, then I wish you the best of luck because this might be a suicide mission."

"And you're just going to send us on our merry way?" Thomas asked, incredulous.

"Yeah, why not? The choice is yours. You're adults. Far be it from me to stop you from fighting supernatural beings when you're clearly outnumbered. Just because it's been a long time since I had a request like this doesn't mean it's the first time. The last guys succeeded without an ounce of magical power between the two of them."

"Care to elaborate on that story?" Thomas asked.

"No," Rhun answered simply. He turned his focus to the water where he began chanting a spell in a language foreign to Vivian. He was working arcane magic. The language of the Ancients, a craft she'd only read about, which was still considered legend even by some of the most notable witches practicing today.

The three of them stood a safe distance behind Rhun as he worked his borrowed ancient magic. She now understood why certain supernaturals might find that so offensive. After a few moments, the marsh began to swirl in a surreal separation from the rest of the land like an oil painting that had a jar of thinner spilled onto the canvas.

"That should do it," Rhun said, stepping back to admire his handiwork. "Feel free to jump in whenever you're ready."

"Jump in?" Thomas's eyes rivaled those of the deer they'd seen on their way driving in.

"Is this guy human or some kind of wereparrot?" Rhun whispered to Vivian.

Vivian smiled, but there were more serious matters at hand. "How do we get back?"

"I'll leave a light on for you," Rhun answered. He offered no further explanation, as she was quickly learning to be his way.

She let out a nervous breath. "Here goes then. Ready guys?"

"Oh, I'm not going," Aubrey corrected.

Vivian raised a questioning eyebrow at him.

"If I didn't make it back, there's someone who would miss me," he said. "Plus, someone has to run the shop."

"Suit yourself." Vivian shrugged. "But if things go south then there might not be a shop to run anyway."

She took Thomas by the hand, more for moral support than necessity.

They jumped together and fell through the veil between dimensions.

Chapter Twelve

Infiltration

Chris's coordinates not only brought Vincent and Marcus straight to the Order's HQ but landed them right inside the building. Although, Vincent already knew the Order's location from the short time he had worked with them but bringing that up to Ethan probably wouldn't have won him any points for his poor allegiance making in the past.

As much as he was heartbroken, he couldn't deny Chris's interference happened to be a godsend. He suspected the Order would have banned the entry spell he'd been allowed to use in the past. It had been years since he'd seen Karen; their son's entire lifetime. And all that time she had thought him dead. Her heartbreak was worse than his. She'd had years of grieving and raising Ethan all on her own. Of course, by now it would be completely understandable she'd moved on. But that didn't make the fact any less crushing.

However, thanks to Karen's new love interest, they were precisely where they needed to be and hadn't done anything yet to call attention to their presence. They had a real shot at succeeding because infiltration was something Vincent did quite well.

Apparently, gaining access to secret organizations was also a specialty Marcus shared, which seemed to be a common thread in their acquaintance. He might have remarked along those lines but Marcus was on his knees next to him appearing quite more like the dead thing he really was.

"Not used to transporting yet?"

"It's not that." Marcus's words were labored. "I haven't eaten anything in days... maybe even a week." He struggled to bring himself back to a standing position. "I may need your help to see this through."

Realizing what he'd implied, Vincent took a step back. "You don't seriously think I'd do that for you?"

"It's the only way I'll have enough strength."

"I still have the option to do this by myself. I could leave you for dead the same way you did me and just tell everyone the Order got you."

Marcus showed his fangs. "I wonder what Ethan would think if he heard you say that. I could just as easily take what I want and drain you."

"But you wouldn't."

"Wouldn't I? You're the only thing keeping me from Dacey, are you not?"

Dangerous tension rose between them. Marcus had to be legitimately insane or in the process of being driven that way from lack of sustenance.

"He's Mercury now. You should probably keep reminding yourself of that." Vincent changed his tone, as though he were dealing with a captive lion only moments from realizing it could break free.

"And what about you?" Marcus took a threatening step forward. "Do you intend to stay yourself or will you join him? Sandman..."

The lion was injured. Vincent saw it now. Marcus had been limping through existence at this point without Dacey. He wasn't trying to break free from anything; he was lashing out because he'd been backed into a corner.

"You don't really care about any of this do you?" Vincent's question was hypothetical. The pain in Marcus's eyes told him everything he needed to know. He knew because he'd been there, betrayed and on the verge of giving up. He wasn't entirely sure he wasn't still at that point himself.

"Why should I?" Marcus retracted his fangs. "No matter what happens, I've already lost the only thing that mattered."

"So, why are you helping them?" Vincent wanted to hear the answer if only to hear the echo of his own thoughts brought to validation.

"Because Dacey—*Mercury* asked me to."

His answer rang sincere, and though simple, Vincent could feel the immense weight of the statement. Was he not doing this himself for the same reason?

"Vincent doesn't exist anymore." He let his guard down. "Figuratively speaking, anyway. I have my son again but... Nothing will ever be the same and I have no idea where any of this will take me. We might not even survive the next few minutes. But I'll make something clear. Whatever Sandman and Mercury had or were... doesn't exist anymore either. That was ages ago. And it doesn't change what remains real between you and Dacey, just like it doesn't change what I feel for Karen. Even if you hadn't tried to knock me off two decades ago, I think we both know I would also be destined to lose out."

"So, what do we, the discarded hearts, do then?"

"The same thing we've always done. We keep going. Because losing isn't always useless." Vincent rolled up his sleeve and offered himself.

Marcus turned to him with an expression of renewed spirit and mutual understanding. Less aggressive, he showed his fangs and took the offering, sinking his bite deep into Vincent's veins. Vincent bit back an instinctive reaction to pull away from the pain and forced himself to give in, letting Marcus suck as much blood out of him as he needed.

He suspected Marcus of taking more than necessary, but he didn't try to stop him. His fangs massaging Vincent's pierced tissue and the small flicks of Marcus's tongue as he nursed the life out of him felt morbidly good. Vincent imagined him as a serpent working in reverse to free the venom of existence from his body. He grew lightheaded.

Marcus must have sensed this because he pulled away and turned around to clean his face off on a handkerchief he produced from his pocket. When he faced Vincent again, he appeared revitalized. As handsome, youthful, and now determined as ever.

"Perhaps I could learn to love again?" Marcus gave a wry smirk.

"I'm not that desperate." Vincent pulled his sleeve back down.

Focusing, Vincent could still hear the disruptor in his subconscious beckoning him to its location. The device had to be somewhere beneath them.

"We need to go down," he advised.

"If that's your litmus test for love, then I'm more than happy to oblige."

Vincent pointed to the floor. "The disruptor. It's somewhere below us."

"Ah." Marcus nodded. "Yes. Best get to it then."

Vincent worried if he'd made the right decision in his spontaneous alliance, but there wasn't much time for second guessing things. They took the nearest hallway and went on a search for the capability of decent.

*

Thomas turned a full circle as though that would somehow right his inner compass. "I thought I was out of my comfort zone during the sleep spell. But no. It's now. Somewhere over there was the zone, and this is me, completely disassociated from it."

The spell had landed them inside a building which was a peculiar mix of old-world brick and mortar but heavily updated with modern, magical, technology. It was a safe assumption they'd breached the Order's headquarters.

He turned to Vivian for confirmation, but she stood still with her eyes closed, muttering.

"Viv? Are you okay?" He rushed to her side in case something had gone wrong.

She held up a hand, indicating she was fine. After a moment, her eyes fluttered open.

"I cast a locator spell." She smiled. "It must have worked because I can feel exactly where we need to go to find Chris."

"That seems a little dangerous," Thomas cautioned. "I mean, don't you think these guys will notice intruders using magic?"

"We have limited resources right now, and magic is pretty much the only thing in our toolbox. This way," she instructed, taking off without giving Thomas an extra moment to question her actions.

"Wait." He leaned forward and grabbed her wrist. "I need to know where the disruptor is."

"You're not seriously thinking of separating." Vivian gawked.

"I told you," he reminded her. "Shutting that thing down sounded like the most helpful thing we could do. I let you pull me into an entirely different dimension. I'm not going to play sidekick in a rescue mission where I'm not even needed. Since I'm here, I might as well do something to make a difference. Implant a locator spell in me, if that's possible. Something to guide me."

"I don't like this." Vivian bit her bottom lip.

"I haven't liked any of this since the moment you told me about your vision," Thomas scoffed. "But I've gone along with everything, and now is our chance to take action and make all of this really count. You know I'm right. We can solve both problems. It'll be the nicest thing I've ever done for Grady."

Vivian chuckled. "It would be the only nice thing you've ever done for him."

"Even more of a reason for you to let me do this." He tried his best to persuade her with puppy dog eyes.

Vivian nodded and closed her eyes again, murmuring. She cast another spell, and this time she placed her palms on his temples. It didn't take long for the magic to start working. Energy jolted through his body like a sudden wave of turbulence. A pull. Something inside him yearned to fall through the floor.

"I know where it is," he confirmed as she opened her eyes again and let him go.

"When you're ready to head back, look for Rhun's signal," Vivian reminded him. "I love you."

She gave him a deep, quick kiss and pulled back to gaze into his eyes. He knew she meant this wasn't goodbye.

He brushed his thumb across her cheek. "I love you too."

Without another word, they took off in opposite directions.

*

"What the shit is this?"

Exasperated, Chase let his cloak fall to the floor unceremoniously. He noticed the silent alarms going off in his quarters. He'd just entered, in hopes of having a moment to himself to regroup and strategize, and now it seemed they were under attack.

After the encounter he'd just had, it would be tempting to let Vid fend for himself with the intruders, but his curiosity got the best of him. Ultimately, anyone who was Vid's enemy would be a problem for him as well. He switched the monitor on his wall to security mode and isolated the intruder's location.

"Idiots." He smirked. There appeared to be only two of them, and they were using a continuous spell which had set off the alarms. They had made themselves moving targets.

"But how did you get in?" He scanned for vulnerability on the exterior of the building but couldn't find any indication of a breach which would mean they had somehow appeared from inside the building. One moved down a corridor of little importance, but the other seemed to be making a beeline for Vid's lair. He assumed it could only mean a sandman was in their midst.

"Well, that didn't take long."

Chase hesitated. He knew he should alert Vid in case he hadn't already noticed the break-in himself. But what he *should* do and what he *would* do had seldom been the same thing.

Fuck him. Chase cast off Vid. *I'll capture the Sandman myself. We'll see how important Vid is when I prove his leadership inconsequential.*

Chapter Thirteen

Mr. Sandman

Vincent and Marcus hit a dead end inside the Order's headquarters. Vincent figured that was a good indicator they were exactly where they needed to be.

"Secret passageways. My favorite cliché," Marcus remarked.

Vincent ran his hands across the wall to feel for any seams.

"Trust me." Marcus nudged him out of the way. "This will be more advanced. Alchemists love illusions."

They'd allowed Marcus to tag along for a reason, so Vincent made room for him to do what he did best.

Marcus went to work on puzzling out whatever magic held them back from their destination.

Vincent grew impatient and paranoid, hearing footsteps in the distance.

"I've almost got it," Marcus reassured. Either he'd heard them too, or he could sense Vincent's anxiousness.

"Almost isn't fast enough. Someone's here." Vincent grabbed Marcus and pulled him into an even darker corner of the hallway. Thank goodness the Order didn't seem to believe in proper lighting.

A man with dark hair in casual clothing came to an abrupt stop at the wall.

Vincent held his breath, waiting to see if the man knew how to get in. If so, they could ambush him once the entrance opened and finish their mission.

Unfortunately, he seemed just as perplexed as they were by the obstacle.

"Now what?" The man, who appeared to be in his late twenties, threw his hands up in frustration.

"Wait, I know you." Marcus stepped out of the shadows and the man pivoted in surprise to face them.

"Marcus!" Vincent reprimanded, unnecessarily maintaining a hushed voice.

"He's one of Grady's friends," Marcus said.

Vincent left the safety of the alcove and glanced over his shoulder to make sure no one else was around.

"I wouldn't go that far," the man quipped. His eyes narrowed at Marcus.

"I met him at a party once," Marcus said to Vincent.

"So, what are you doing here?" Vincent asked, taking on the role of interrogator so Marcus could get back to work. It was only a matter of time before someone more threatening stumbled upon them.

"I guess the same thing you are. Trying to find a device that's disrupting the Dream World," the man explained as he watched with rapt curiosity while Marcus produced various amulets from his personage and muttered a few incantations at the wall.

The man continued, "Ethan sent my girlfriend here to save someone, but I thought destroying this thing would be a little more important."

"Good call." Vincent let his defenses down a little. He chose to believe him but wasn't a fan of the growing number of unknown variables interfering with what he'd hoped would be a quick mission.

"What's he doing?" The man's eyes widened.

Vincent turned to Marcus, who had just cut his palm open with a pocketknife and wiped what could have been mostly Vincent's blood across the wall.

"Old magic requires old solutions," Marcus explained as the wall disappeared, opening into the entryway to a staircase which descended into an unknown destination.

"Great. Now they have our DNA samples." Vincent brushed past him in a mad rush to find the device before any more precious time was wasted. Their new cohort tagged along behind him.

"I don't think I..." Marcus's mutters were lost to him as Vincent bound down the stairs. There wasn't any point in worrying about being disruptive now. If anyone happened to be down there, they'd already be expecting their arrival anyway. Vincent prepared himself for anything.

He let out a steady breath as they reached the bottom and found the lair empty. In the massive open layout room there weren't many places someone could be hiding. At least not that he could discern.

Modernity seemed to have overgrown simpler times in the strange chamber. The stone walls appeared ancient, but they surrounded a room filled with technology so advanced Vincent felt like he'd traveled back to the ghost galaxy. A chill went up his spine as he wondered how many other sandmen had entered this same lair and not come out alive.

Although he'd had every intention of immediately locating the disruptor, Vincent became drawn to a glass case across the room so massive it commanded immediate attention.

As they wandered in, Vincent made his way over to the case. He got the sense it must be more than just a standard container but suspected it wasn't the disruptor. A smokey translucent haze swirled across the surface area of the gigantic cube, and he realized, once close enough to touch, the essence was trapped inside the glass. If the case was even glass at all.

"I wouldn't get too close," Marcus advised from across the room. "Remember what I said about alchemists and their illusions."

Vincent couldn't help himself, though, and he placed his palm against the pane. A sudden familiar feeling swept through him, as though he'd been here before. For a split second, he thought a cloudy face overlapped his reflection in the glass. Unnerved, he let go of the case and took a cautious step back.

"I'm going to go out on a limb and guess this is it," the man with the dark hair said.

Vincent turned toward the man and realized they'd never traded names. But now wasn't the time for proper introductions either. The man stood right next to the disruptor, which sat questionably unattended next to the Sandman Codex atop an altar. An obvious trap.

He had the horrible feeling they'd done precisely what the Order had wanted them to.

*

Chris wasn't locked in the lab, so when the pounding fists against the glass window on the door sounded, he jolted with surprise out of his deep focus on the intricate design he'd been manufacturing.

He lifted his magnifying spectacle and set his instruments down as soon as he noticed the frantic woman trying to get his attention. She didn't seem like a member of the Order. They were usually much more disturbingly calm and overdressed. It took a moment for her face to register, but he eventually recognized her from the photos in Grady's office. Vivian Edwards, his friend's former secretary.

How the hell...?

"It's unlocked!" he called out. He acted out an awkward mimic of opening the door.

She must not have been able to hear him because she started what appeared to be the beginning of a spell.

"No, no, no!" He dashed over, waving frantically for her to stop. Obviously, she was here without permission from the Order and any use of magic would give her whereabouts away. He yanked the door open, much to her confusion.

"I—I thought you were trapped," she said as she entered the lab.

"Well, I am. You know. In the grand scheme of things," he confirmed. "But not to this room in particular."

"Oh." Her eyes widened as she assessed the magnitude of the technology working in conjunction with magical instruments. Her gaze eventually rested back on him, "Ethan sent me to save you."

"Ugh!" Exasperated, Chris's shoulders slumped, and he rolled his head to the side, which lead into his pivot and stride back to the desk where he'd been working at a feverish pace. "That's exactly what I didn't want him to do. I said, *destroy the disruptor*. Why are instructions so hard for supernaturals? Must have something to do with the fact that they exist between the lines to begin with."

"Don't worry about the disruptor." She stood next to him, scrutinizing his work. "My boyfriend is taking care of it."

"Well, that's a relief. What kind of creature is he?"

"A human."

Chris paused, trying to find the silver lining. "But a human with paranormal abilities, right?"

"He has a degree in Veterinary Science," she offered.

Chris rolled his eyes. "Great. At least Benny will make it out of this mess alive. I'll begin rejoicing forthwith. Hold this, will you? And try not to drop them. They're explosive."

He handed her what appeared to be a couple of small gears.

"What is all this?" She leaned closer for a better look at the two small metallic hoops in front of him.

"In theory? A safeguard." He finished soldering on the panels and then indicated he wanted the gears. She handed them back with care. Once one was secured inside each cuff, he screwed the panels on.

"They look like bracelets," she observed.

He knew she wanted him to elaborate, but they had no time to spare.

"Hopefully, your boyfriend succeeds, but just in case, I think we should provide some backup." Chris gathered up the cuffs and nodded for her to follow him.

"You're a witch, right? Grady told me."

"Yes." She kept pace with him as they left the lab.

"You any good with binding spells?"

*

Vincent, Marcus, and the man who had joined them stood over the disruptor in the underground chamber. Vincent leaned forward to scope out the device, impressed by its simplicity of design considering its complex capabilities.

"So, what do we do? Just smash it or something?" Their tagalong surveyed the room for any club-like object that might do the trick.

"I would think it'll be a bit more difficult than that," Marcus weighed in. "Vincent might need to take care of this."

He held out his hand, in an *after-you* motion and stood back.

Vincent rolled his shoulders back and held out his arms, palms facing the device. His body began to glow with dream energy.

"I've been waiting so long for this little family reunion, *cousin*." A voice interrupted, "Marcus, grab him!"

Without hesitation, the vampire latched onto Vincent from behind and pinned his arms against his sides.

A redheaded man in a suit and tie emerged from the shadows.

"Who are you?" Marcus demanded, though he still held Vincent tight on the stranger's command.

"Chase." Vincent recognized him from his previous work with the Order.

"I'm here in Vid's stead," Chase explained to Marcus. "And actually, the disruptor *could* be smashed, so I'm glad you hesitated."

Marcus let out a disgruntled growl but continued to restrain Vincent.

How could I be stupid enough to trust him twice?

Thank goodness for their newly made mortal friend because he wasted no time in the moment seizing his chance to grab the device and hurtle it against the wall, shattering the damned thing into a hundred little pieces.

Chase frowned. "That was unwise."

"Run!" Vincent urged him.

The man took off for the staircase, but a wall of flames stopped him from being able to exit. The fire circled around him, trapping him in one spot. Vincent took a moment to register that Chase had produced the blaze right out of his hands.

"When did you start practicing pyromancy?" Desperate, Vincent scrambled to think of ways to buy time until he could come up with an escape plan.

He ignored his question. "It's nice to see you again, Vincent. After, you know, everyone thought you'd died," Chase said with smugness. "All I'm saying is a postcard would've been nice."

"Where's Vid? I demand to speak with him!" Marcus snarled.

"How about you help me put our friend Vincent inside the magic box, and then I'll fetch Vid for you." Chase indicated the large glass prism Vincent had inspected earlier.

Vincent fought against Marcus's grip but like a torture device, his struggles only caused the vampire to hold on to him tighter. Against his will, Marcus began to walk him toward the glass prison. He only now realized his huge mistake in letting Marcus drink from him. With sandman blood fueling him, he could match Vincent's strength.

"What is that thing?" Vincent demanded as Chase joined them by the tank.

"Well, it's custom built just for you." He produced another evil smirk and patted the glass. "You've seen sand in an hourglass. Think of this as a Sandman in a cube. But wait! There's more!"

He said the latter like a cheesy gameshow host and loped into an enthusiastic trot over to a large sheet covering an object the same size a few feet away. Continuing his mockery, he yanked the sheet off causing the fabric to flutter down and reveal a similar encasement. On this one, however, the glass filled with a darker and more murky liquid.

"Behind door number two, a prison for Mercury, as well!" he announced, overpleased with himself. "That slippery, meddlesome traitor will finally be under control. Meant to be a messenger, never meant to be our equal. He'll learn his place in the universe. I can't wait to educate him on submission."

Marcus's grip on Vincent slackened. Perhaps not everything Marcus had said had been a complete lie after all. *Aha, a chance for escape.* Vincent tried his best to not relax his body in any form that would indicate to the vampire he wasn't holding on quite as tight as he needed to.

"I'm sorry, what?" Marcus sounded unsure of himself.

Chase's indignant smile faltered, but he tried to maintain the composure of control.

"Just get the sandman in the box, and I'll explain everything."

"There's no need." Vid now emerged from the shadows. "I'll take it from here."

Marcus tightened his grip again, but Vincent suspected this time his reaction came from possessiveness and not deference to Chase.

"Vid, looks like you're the liar I always expected you to be." Marcus accused. "When you came to me you said this would be an even exchange. A sandman for Dacey."

"Yes, and you were the one to backtrack on that deal," Vid revealed. "You cut off contact and tried to take the young sandman as your own."

"And why wouldn't I?" Marcus challenged. "If all I needed was a sandman to get Dacey back, then I would've been perfectly capable of achieving that on my own. I had no idea why either one was important to you. You'd long been trying to get Dacey to leave me. Why would I now believe you wanted to fetch him back? I didn't know him to be Mercury then; you obviously chose to leave the finer details out. I don't appreciate people attempting to manipulate me. The truth is Dacey is never coming back. Just like you're never getting Sandman."

"Hand over Sandman, and I'll make certain Phantom provides a way to bring your precious Dacey back." Vid tried to tempt him.

Chase gritted his teeth. "Why are you lowering yourself to placate him? He's a useless vampire. This is precisely why you're so weak."

"Weak? How dare you speak to me with such insubordination!"

It was a split second of hate-fueled distraction between the two alchemists but both Marcus and Vincent recognized their opportunity.

Marcus released Vincent and made a run for the Codex, snatching the tome off the altar.

Vincent created a shield of dream energy to part the firewall holding their comrade hostage.

"Thomas!" A woman's voice cried out as she descended the stairs with a man with blue hair.

At least now I know his name, Vincent thought as Thomas broke free to join the newcomers. Once reunited, Vincent turned toward the chaos.

A loud crack rang out as Marcus slammed Chase against Mercury's prospective prison. Vincent wasn't sure if the break came from Chase's bones or the cube. With a vampire's strength of force boosted by his sandman blood, the noise could easily be either or both.

The impact didn't slow the alchemist down one bit though. He gripped Marcus by the throat with rage. "I can turn you to ash in a second!"

"Stop this at once!" Vid attempted to intervene by casting a spell that forced the two apart. He bellowed, "Your narrow vision will ruin everything!"

"Your cowardice is the Order's ruin!" Chase produced a whip of fire, which shot out and wrapped around Vid, constricting and consuming him in a blaze. Vid attempted to chant his way to freedom, but the fire wound its way up and forced flames inside his mouth and throat.

The chamber filled with muffled, terrified screams.

Horrified, Vincent ran toward the others on the stairwell. "Do you have a safe way to escape?"

"I think so," the woman answered. Her assumption would have to be good enough.

"Then go!" he urged them before they became Chase's next target.

She turned to the blue-haired man for a response.

"I'll be fine. He's right, you two get out of here."

Thomas took her hand, and the two ascended the stairs while Chase still had his back to them.

Vid fell to the ground, nothing more than a charred image of his former self.

Chase rounded on the remaining three before they could even attempt to make a move.

"Your turn." He grinned wickedly in Marcus's direction.

"What is this betrayal?" a cavernous voice sounded as the highest-ranking members of The Order appeared from the shadows.

Chase straightened his posture and greeted them with confident conviction. "Cousins! Welcome to a new era! The return of Dawn. Earth's rebirth!"

"You've murdered him," Lauma, the Fae, accused.

"Vid's sacrifice is a prelude to greater things. Summon Phantom!" Chase commanded and then turned their attention to Vincent and the rest. "The Sandman's vessel has arrived."

Their gazes fell on Vincent, and he could sense their appraisal. The suspicion they had dissipated and morphed into vindicated excitement.

"This can't be good," Vincent muttered. Marcus came to stand beside him, in a protective stance, as though he hadn't just admitted being a traitor.

"It most assuredly isn't," Marcus concurred. "I deeply regret my involvement."

"Oh, I'm sure you do." Vincent oozed sarcasm.

The blue-haired man stepped up behind them and whispered, "Hi, I'm Chris. Mind if I take it from here?"

"Be our guest," Vincent said. He regarded Chris with intent interest, now that he knew his identity with certainty.

Chris activated the cuff devices and made for a quick run at Chase. Out of the shadows, a jackalope appeared, causing Vincent to wonder how many more of the Order were going to shadow walk in. He needed to transport them out of here fast.

The massive creature caught up to Chris before he had a chance to make his move and gave him a hefty kick backward with such force that Chris went flying into Marcus. The two tumbled to the ground.

"Time to go, fellas." Vincent pivoted to get nearer to them so he could take them back to the Dream World.

Vincent shouted in pain as a wave of burning flames overcame him. The wide-eyed expressions on both Marcus's and Chris's faces let him know what he feared to be true. Chase had set him on fire.

He tried to morph the flames off and push a shield of dream energy out as a layer to protect himself, but Chase's attacks were unrelenting. He reached out to Marcus for help, though he knew there wasn't time for anyone to save him. He couldn't breathe, and the pain was too severe. The bright fire consumed him so he couldn't see anything else anymore. He fell and gave in to the hungry flames.

His eyes flew open again. He was still on fire, but he no longer hurt. He felt nothing. He stood and, effortlessly, managed to cause the flames to die out with a forceful push of dream energy more intense than any he'd ever been able to summon before.

He knew the truth before seeing the proof from his own body. He'd become a shell of pure dream matter, radiant and glowing. He'd transmutated. Vincent had died and Sandman had returned.

He turned to face Chase and the other Elementals who stood in momentary awe of his presence.

A loud groan echoed through the chamber. Everyone's attention drew back to Vid's charred corpse.

"The final portal has been opened!" Chase announced. His triumphant grin seemed inhumanly wide and monstrous.

A billowing black veil of stardust began to flow out of Vid's lifeless mouth. The energy wound its way around the chamber until the room was cloaked in a blanket of night. A haunting echo of maniacal laughter surrounded them until finding its target and reformed into a large and menacing shadow man who stood facing Sandman.

The incident had summoned Death himself. Mercury now stood between Sandman and the remaining High Council.

"What have you done?" It was as though Mercury were insinuating their failure had been Sandman's fault.

Sandman's heart sank. The moment their past selves had tried so hard to prevent had found a way to transpire regardless of their efforts. He clenched his jaw and acknowledged his brother.

"Phantom."

Chapter Fourteen

Dreamscape

"Last time we came here, I pretty much died. Are you sure this is the best idea?" Ethan knew it was too late to ask. They were already in Nightmare's realm, waiting for him to acknowledge their presence.

"Considering Nightmare is the only other Celestial who wields arcane dream magic and hasn't abandoned this corner of the multiverse, I believe this is the final valid idea I have." Ethan sensed a hint of uncertainty in Mercury's statement, but good idea or not, they couldn't back out now. Nightmare had arrived.

"Back so soon?" Nightmare smirked.

"Things are...hairier than expected," Mercury admitted.

"Aren't they always?" Nightmare grinned, and a chill ran up Ethan's spine. His amusement morphed to frustration. "I heard the message your friend put out. That disruptor has been keeping me from my work."

"It's taken care of," Mercury assured him. "In the meantime, I was hoping you could teach Ethan how to— oh, I don't know—create another dimension within the Dream World?"

Nightmare let out a hearty laugh.

"Is that even possible?" Up until this point, Ethan hadn't been sure what Mercury's plan was, but now he questioned his sanity even more so than usual.

"It is possible," Nightmare revealed. "Also, dangerous. Not to mention forbidden." He eyed Mercury with suspicion.

"Really? Do we know for certain than anyone is even upholding the Old Laws anymore?" Mercury asked. "I mean, I've seen numerous infractions in the last twenty-four hours alone."

"What happens if you break an Old Law?" Ethan wondered. He remembered reading a few passages in his father's and Arthur's book about sleep travel that mentioned forbidden things.

"What generally happens in mythology when someone defies the gods?" Mercury asked.

Ethan's throat tightened at the thought.

"Anyway, I wouldn't be so concerned with the cosmic straight and narrow. Anyone can see what we're seeking to do, considering what's at stake, is entirely within reason and wholly altruistic."

"I doubt wholly." Nightmare dismissed Mercury's input and turned his attention to Ethan. "But still a considerably hazardous undertaking. You could remain trapped in a dreamscape for eternity."

The prospect terrified Ethan but he remembered he'd prepared for something similar before.

"I have an anchor," he said. "If anything happens to me, tell Grady. He'll know what to do."

Taken aback, Nightmare demanded, "You entrust your life to a mortal?"

"I do."

Mercury smiled in triumph as Nightmare seemed to take a moment for that fact to sink in and settle with him.

"Isn't the new guard just darling?" Mercury pressed.

"I will help you," Nightmare finally agreed. "But only because I have some unfinished business with Phantom. Seeing him fail wouldn't displease me."

"Pettiness has been the key to most progress, historically speaking. We're glad to hear you're on board." Mercury spoke in a hurried tone. "Now, let's get to it, shall we?"

A loud crack sounded somewhere in the aether, and the same electric jolt of awareness must have resonated through all of them as they regarded one another with disturbed clarity.

Phantom had been freed from exile.

"Bugger." Mercury allowed his scythe to appear, tapped it once hard against the ground, and disappeared.

Without warning, Nightmare unhinged his jaws, opening his mouth into a surreal and immense abyss and swallowed Ethan whole.

*

Ethan's eyes fluttered open. He yawned, staring up at the rhythmic movement of the fan blades above his couch. His throw pillow had somehow released itself from behind his head and he cuddled it tight against his chest.

The sun barged in through the cracks in the blinds, so he knew he'd overslept.

Great. Another missed class I'll have to come up with an excuse for. He'd have to invest in a real alarm clock and quit relying on his phone if he didn't want to end up flunking out of college.

Exhausted because every muscle in his body hurt as though he'd run a marathon the day before, he forced himself to face the day. He swung his legs off the couch and sat up; all his memories came rushing back to him.

Grady, the gigantic werewolf, vampires, and his father. All of it. His heart caught up with his thoughts, pounding, panic overtaking him. Why was he back in his old apartment? Why were all his things still here? He'd moved out months ago.

A terrible realization washed over him.

"No. No, no, no, no!" He jumped up, still in his clothes from the day before. The day he'd gone in for his interview with Dr. Grady Hunter. He slid his shoes on with urgency and opened his phone's contact list to call Grady. He typed the name, but nothing pulled up. He began furiously scrolling, which didn't take long since he didn't have many friends, and came to the horrific conclusion he no longer had his number. In full blown panic mode, he searched for Dacey's number next and found nothing.

His memories were so surreal, but he'd die of heartbreak if the truth was anything less than reality.

There was only one sure way to find out. He grabbed his bike and took off, peddling so hard that he could feel every inch of his body burning with exertion. He made his way through town and to Grady's office. At least, where his office should have been. The building seemed exactly as he remembered but now sat vacant with a real estate sign posted in the front.

Not believing his own eyes, he dropped the bike and ran to the glass doors, pressing as close as he could to get a good look inside. The place was empty and appeared as though it had been vacant for a long period of time.

Was he going mad? *Maybe this is a dream.* He pinched himself. It hurt.

Feeling desperate, he pulled his phone out again and called Arthur.

After two rings, his familiar voice picked up.

"Good morning." He sounded a bit accusatory.

"Arthur!" Ethan didn't see a point in hiding his desperation. "Where is Grady?"

"I'm sorry, who?"

"Grady!" Ethan pleaded, "Grady Hunter! His office is gone. Do you know where he's at? It's important!"

"Ethan, you sound upset. Is everything all right? I know you missed class today."

"Just tell me where he is!"

"I'm sorry, but I have no idea who you're talking about."

Ethan refused to believe what became more and more apparent. "Of course you do! He's your friend! You sent me to meet with him."

"Ethan, you're worrying me. Should I come by to check on you?"

No. This isn't happening. Hot tears of frustration and sorrow welled up in his eyes. Ethan hung up on Arthur, seeing no point in torturing himself with their conversation any longer.

Determined, he wiped the tears away and grabbed his bike again. There was one more place he could check. One last bit of hope his memories hadn't all just been a dream.

The ride took longer than he would have liked. About halfway through, he thought maybe if he'd allowed himself to calm down a bit, then he would have had the sense to catch an Uber or call Arthur back and ask to use his car.

He also thought maybe, subconsciously, he'd wanted to take the longer route as a defense. To prolong the illusion before facing the depressing fact Grady, and everything else, had been a figment of his overactive imagination. That prospect was too dark a thought to accept. Now that he'd known Grady, he couldn't imagine a life without him. He'd rather face a thousand more celestial monsters than to take one more breath of air in a world where Grady didn't exist.

A world where he wasn't a sandman.

He eventually made it to Grady's manor right about the time he realized he could test his own theory by attempting to use his powers.

To his relief, there was no real estate sign anywhere in sight. Unfortunately, the house appeared just as abandoned as the office space. He leaned his bike against the last lamp post that lined Grady's driveway and hurried to the door to ring the bell.

He waited a good deal longer than anyone normally would in hopes someone was there and just taking their time to come to answer. After a while, he rang the bell over and over and resumed waiting.

Ethan couldn't hear any movement from inside, but the longer he stood there, the more he got the sense he wasn't alone. He could feel someone's gaze burning into the back of his head. He hoped maybe it was Agatha.

Instinctively, he turned around. There was no one else there, but he did notice some movement in the overgrown grass, and he knew there wasn't a breeze.

Giving up on hoping anyone might be inside, he made his way with caution down the steps and toward the movement. Whatever was there stopped moving when he stood within several feet. A tiny growl emanated from the brush.

His heart jumped at the familiar sound.

"Benny?" He knelt to show he meant no harm. "Benny! Is that you?"

The growling stopped, replaced by a curious whimper. Moments later, out of the tall grass, stepped a tiny brown chihuahua.

Ethan's voice choked with joy. "You have no idea how glad I am to see you!"

He wasn't sure if the dog had any real idea of who he was, but his overjoyed greeting obviously excited him, and Benny's tail began wildly wagging. He ran over and jumped around Ethan, trying to get a few good licks in.

Ethan pet him and gave him a hug of appreciation.

"I hope you remember me," he said once the chihuahua had calmed down enough to stand somewhat still with his tongue lolling out as he caught his breath.

His wagging tail was the only hope Ethan had left. Or so he thought, until he remembered one other thing he could try.

Standing again, he reached out and summoned everything within himself. To his immense satisfaction, he emitted a pulse of blue dream energy that shot out of his palms and across the yard, dissipating as it hit the wall of the manor.

Benny let out another curious whimper and cocked his head to the side.

"It wasn't a dream," Ethan surmised. "So where is everyone?"

He turned to Benny as though he could possibly answer.

"Wait. It's daytime. Shouldn't you be human right now?"

The dog yawned, obviously growing bored of his new friend and sat down to stare at nothing down the driveway as all real dogs are generally wont to do.

A new hypothesis began to formulate as Ethan remembered what had happened to him right before he'd woken up in this weird alternate state.

"It wasn't a dream," he puzzled aloud. The chihuahua seemed intrigued by him again as though he were now the one searching for answers.

"This is real, but so was everything else." Ethan kept working the situation out. "This is the dreamscape Nightmare knew I could create."

The one Mercury wants me to pull Phantom into. The immensity of his task overtook him. Unsure of how much time he'd wasted since Phantom's arrival, he knew he'd have to get creative and fast.

"Benny, I really need you to not be a dog right now."

Benny offered a bark of apology.

"Wait," Ethan realized. "You're not the real Benny."

Benny growled as if offended.

"And if you're not really the real Benny because I realized you into being Benny, then that means maybe I can realize the real Benny into you."

Benny whimpered in confusion and lay down as though critical analysis were all too tiring for a small chihuahua to have the energy for.

Wild ideas were percolating in Ethan's imagination, and to test them out he faced the manor.

"If this is a dreamscape I've created, then I can do anything here. I should be able to manipulate every facet," he continued explaining to Benny. Though, the exposition was more for his own benefit as he wrapped his head around the surreal powers he held as a sandman.

With focus and not nearly as much effort as he'd imagined it would take, he lifted the manor off the ground. As the house levitated, he commanded each brick to slide in and out of place, allowing the structure to reconfigure itself.

As startled as any dog would be, Benny hopped up and began running in circles, barking wildly at the rogue household.

The facade of the manor became unrecognizable as the architecture morphed into a small fortress, then into a castle, then into a dragon. Ethan had to fight the urge to keep creating things. Who wouldn't want to fight a battle with a dragon on their side? But he knew fantasy elements would break the illusion he would have to create to fool Phantom. Ethan needed him to think they were on Earth, not in a controlled bubble.

He set the dragon down and turned the creature back into the manor.

Ethan turned to Benny. "Your turn."

Benny whined and pivoted to run away.

Ethan anchored himself, closed his eyes, and let his essence travel back to the Dream World where he showed up in Kit's dwelling in full Sandman form.

*

Being left behind to rally and prepare the weakest of their group wasn't exactly the part Grady had pictured himself playing in a battle on a stage as large as this. He didn't want to seem insensitive or pretentious, but he deemed himself quite overqualified for his current assignment. He felt frustratingly useless.

Of course, he cared deeply about the people he was protecting, but he'd much rather be at Ethan's side. There was no telling what Mercury had wrangled him into.

All Grady had managed to do was get caught up in an unsolicited game of twenty questions from Benny, which had not ended at the usual twenty, and he grew more and more impatient and worried about Ethan as time wore on.

"What's that?" Benny stopped the anxious pacing routine he had taken up as soon as Grady had arrived with the news.

Grady, leaning against a wall, had only been paying halfhearted attention to Benny's whirlwind of worries while Arthur and Karen were making peace with the fact that everyone agreed they should remain behind for their own safety. They weren't happy feeling removed from the situation either and Benny's incessant questions were making Karen nervous. She and Arthur had excused themselves out of the room some time ago. Only Kit remained with them, and her positive enthusiasm was doing little to help either. She'd insisted Benny should join them in battle, which propelled him into interrogating Grady on the various possibilities and probabilities of doggy death in a supernatural war zone.

Grady sighed with exasperation, considering a nap at this point. He admitted, "I don't know. I stopped listening to you several minutes ago."

Offended, Benny frowned and crossed his arms. Then he pointed behind Grady and clarified, "I meant *that*."

Grady turned to see a blue humanoid figure made of swirling starlight and recognized Ethan's sandman form in a heartbeat. Overjoyed his silent plea for involvement had been answered, he stood with purpose again.

"Ethan! What's happened?"

"That's Ethan?" Benny's nose twitched as though he were sniffing out the proof. "Why does he look like a giant tube of glitter glue?"

"I'm a sandman, remember?" Ethan, kind enough to explain in order to get Benny's, currently metaphorical, hackles down. "It's like when you're a chihuahua doing dog things. This is just what I look like when I'm doing sandman things."

"Yes, and what sandman things are you up to at the moment exactly?" Grady interjected.

"It's a little complicated. Okay, it's insanely complicated," Ethan admitted. "But I think I know how to deal with Phantom. And I need you three to help me in order to do it."

It seemed as if the universe was placating Grady in that moment. Then he wondered what had happened to everyone else. "What about Mercury and Vincent? And Marcus?"

"I have to trust Mercury has everything else handled," Ethan explained, keeping things vague. "But this is the path Nightmare sent me on, and I just need you to trust me."

Staying true to his loyal canine roots, Benny answered first. "We're in."

Kit scratched behind his ear with approval, causing Benny to produce a proud goofy smile.

Emboldened, Grady nodded to Ethan, ready to do whatever would be necessary.

"So, what's the plan?"

Chapter Fifteen

Dream Weaver

Hidden, Mercury observed the confrontation from the shadows of the chamber and waited for the opportune moment to act.

"Okay, this is definitely worth documenting for posterity," Chris said, feeling around his body for a recording device.

"At this rate, there won't be any future generations to document it for." Marcus sneered at him. "Didn't you have some sort of useful weapon you were about to use before the Easter bunny hippety-hopped you over the head? Seems to have done some lasting damage."

Chris frowned at him. "I can see why you're not well-liked."

"Who says I'm not well-liked?"

Chris wasn't the only one with an opportunity to seize the moment of tension between the Celestials and make a move. Chase had somehow exited the chamber unnoticed. Everyone's attention set on Phantom.

Chris jogged toward the staircase after Chase, ignoring the looming presence of Harvey the rabbit.

"Where do you think you're going?" Marcus called out while he trotted to the exit.

Mercury finally chose to pop out of the shadows and grabbed Marcus's collar from behind. "I could ask the same about you. How did you let things get so bad? You had one job."

Marcus turned to face Mercury with wide eyes. "I've had multiple jobs since the day I met you."

"I'm sure you'll find it pertinent to enlighten me to them all someday, but for now we need to get this situation contained," Mercury stated with authority.

"What do you suggest?" Marcus asked.

"Mercury?" Sandman had caught sight of him, causing Phantom to take notice as well.

"You're making this far too easy on me." Phantom smiled with a wicked sense of glee.

Mercury turned to Marcus with an apologetic gaze. "My love, please forgive me for this."

Removing a black glove, he placed one of his glowing skeletal fingers in between Marcus's eyes.

Marcus's body shifted like how it had changed in the Dream World. He was mortal again.

Mercury saw the fear in Marcus's eyes as he asked, "Wh-what are you doing?"

"I need you to go to sleep," Mercury explained, his tone soft. "Forever."

He grabbed Marcus by the throat. Marcus struggled to pull himself free, but it was no use. He couldn't overpower Mercury. He couldn't stop Death. But he continued to fight until he gasped his last breath. His spirit released, and his body collapsed to the floor. Marcus hovered above himself, and Mercury read his thoughts as he realized he was no longer connected to it.

Mercury sighed but smiled up at him. "Now you can haunt me forever as you've always wished to do."

Marcus had become a ghost, completely under Death's control.

"Go to Ethan," Mercury instructed.

"My jacket." Marcus's ghostly form nodded down at his body before dissipating from sight.

Mercury bent down to feel the interlining of Marcus's jacket and found the Codex. He tossed the tome to Sandman. "I believe this belongs to you!"

"You've learned some new tricks, I see." Phantom was upon him in an instant.

"Better than turning stale, harping over the old ones," Mercury challenged.

Enraged, Phantom shattered himself into a dozen shadow demons.

"Look out!" Sandman shot a pulse of dream energy their way, trying to hit Phantom in all his separated parts. Phantom must have expected the attack, though, and dodged the strike with precision.

"Nothing to worry about, my love. He forgets he's dealing with Death now," Mercury reminded them both. He honed his own shadow magic to wrangle each shadow demon together and forced Phantom to reform back into himself.

Phantom appeared only a little shocked, mostly frustrated.

"Case in point," Mercury beamed and wiggled his fingers. "New tricks."

Phantom lunged for him, but a sudden lurch in the floor caught him off guard, causing him to lose his balance for a moment.

Mercury, along with the others, became distracted by the room changing itself. The walls appeared to warp and bend like thin sheets of metal being swayed. They all lost their footing as the floor began to wobble as well.

"What is this?" Phantom demanded, turning his full rage back on Sandman.

"It's not me," Sandman insisted, also perplexed.

Mercury couldn't contain his glee. He let out a maniacal laugh that drew unsettled looks from both Phantom and Sandman.

The room around them now began to fade away and morph into someplace else. Someplace outdoors. Somewhere earthy.

"Come on, Phantom, old boy." Mercury grinned, the only one comfortable with their spontaneous unstable surroundings. "You came all this way for a fight, did you not? We're simply headed to a worthy battlefield."

Mercury turned to Sandman. "Leave. Find the Elementals and stop them."

"But—"

"Trust me, love. I know what I'm doing."

Reluctant, Sandman nodded and transported himself away.

The room disappeared in whole by this point, leaving them all exposed and standing in an open field next to a large house Mercury found all too familiar.

"Interesting choice," he muttered to himself, regarding their surroundings.

"So, this is your doing," Phantom accused.

"Not entirely." Mercury pointed in a casual manner past them all to the front stoop of the manor.

Phantom and the others turned to see Ethan, in full sandman form, alongside Grady, Benny, Kit, a ghostly Marcus, and a dozen rallied kitsune.

"We'll call it a group effort," Mercury taunted.

"Where are...?" Phantom whipped around. The loyal servants he'd spent ages enlisting into servitude were nowhere to be found. He'd finally got the showdown he'd been after, but he'd have to fight alone just the same as he had so long ago.

"Sadly, you're not the only megalomaniac in existence." Mercury sized up his concern. "It seems the Elementals had other plans."

Phantom split into fragments of himself again. This time, a hundred shadow demons.

"Stretching yourself a bit thin, wouldn't you say?" Mercury called forth his shadow scythe again and tried to reign in the small spirit army, many of which were already swarming the others at the manor. He could only force a dozen or so at a time back into Phantom's form before they continued to find the strength to escape.

"Death alone could never fully touch me before, and now most certainly cannot." Phantom's voice swirled around Mercury. "You forget. I can no longer be destroyed."

"I've forgotten nothing," Mercury assured as he continued to fend off the shadow demons. Many had already escaped him and were headed toward the group at the manor.

I hope you're as clever as I've given you credit for, Mercury mind-linked with Ethan.

Honestly? I hope so too, Ethan responded.

*

Grady admired the dozen kitsune Ethan had dreamed up to help with the facade on Kit's advice. With their history of loyalty to Sandman, she insisted they'd be the most believable creatures to aid in a fight against Phantom. From Phantom's perspective, they were still far outnumbered by his army of shadow demons.

"Imagine being so disliked and narcissistic that you'd replicate yourself just to have a fan club," Benny said. He stood in defense next to Ethan, Grady, and Kit. He shifted back into chihuahua form and let out a protective growl.

"No need to imagine when it's headed straight for us," Grady said and turned to Ethan. "Care to move forward with our little experiment?"

Ethan gave an assertive nod. They had planned a body switch as another ruse. Grady was the one target Phantom had no reason to care about or keep an eye on. He had no idea who he was and would only recognize him as a human without any supernatural powers of his own. He'd be nothing more than scenery in Phantom's eyes. At least, that's what they were counting on. Ethan could easily move forward with their plan disguised as Grady.

In the meantime, it was up to the others and Grady, disguised as Ethan, to keep Phantom fighting, convinced the battle was real, and he wasn't just being manipulated.

Ethan rested his palms on Grady's temples and concentrated. Manipulating the dreamscape, and everything within, became easier every time he tried. In mere moments, they had switched places with success. Ethan, who now appeared to everyone else as Grady, took off into the manor to keep their plan moving forward.

The shadow demons were on them now, and the imagined dream creatures were putting on a pretty good show in fending them off. Some even disappeared, faking their own deaths.

Benny, surprisingly, took things very seriously. Grady, now in Ethan's body, wondered how hard it must be for a werehuahua to discern reality, but it didn't really matter. He'd be safe no matter what happened here, and the more invested he was in the fight, the more convincing the production would be to Phantom. Benny tried his best to capture and shake the little shadow demons in his jaws, gnawing them like chew toys.

Seeming excited by the prospect of oral torment, Kit followed his lead. She morphed into a kitsune and joined the fray of fur and shadow screeches.

"They make a lovely couple," ghost Marcus remarked. "Reminds me of Dacey and myself in our youth."

"Are you a ghost, or did Sandman find a way to project you here?" The question had been on Grady's mind as soon as Marcus had appeared in the Dream World to tell them that Mercury needed him to summon everyone's subconscious to the dreamscape post haste.

"Oh, yes. I'm quite dead now," Marcus assured. "Honestly, it's not as bad as I thought it would be. Although, I wish I would've had time to pick out my forever outfit a bit more discerningly." He gestured to his simple white button-up which bore a few reminiscing blood stains. "I miss my blue jacket already."

Several shadow demons flew up and attached themselves to the two, biting and clawing at them, attempting to send waves of fear into their hearts.

"Oh, gross!" Marcus tried to brush them off. "Shoo!"

Grady did his best to pretend to be somewhat thwarted and cast small energy shields every now and again to push them back. Using sandman energy was part of the act, playing a convincing Ethan, but he enjoyed having the ability to produce magic. He'd only ever borrowed magical energy before; he'd never imagined what being the source felt like. The sensation was thrilling.

He knew, once Ethan was ready, they would have to find some way to gather all the demons and force Phantom back together again.

"We need to corral these insects closer to Mercury," Grady instructed. He cast a glance in the Celestial's direction. Mercury did his best to gather up the ones he could, but Phantom was only a quarter of the way reformed by Grady's estimate.

"Allow me to borrow your magic." Marcus reached out, expectant.

Grady hesitated.

"Oh, please. What could I possibly do in this current state?" Marcus frowned down at his translucent self.

Grady had taken a lot of leaps of faith at this point, so he decided one more couldn't hurt. He handed over some dream energy.

"I have just as much reason to want revenge as you," Marcus assured him.

"Revenge isn't my motive." Grady found relief speaking the words. For once, the statement rang true.

"To each his own." Marcus shrugged and turned the dream energy into a net. He flew around collecting as many shadow demons as he could.

Following his lead, Grady used the dream energy in a similar fashion, and everyone else did their best to lead whatever shadow demons were terrorizing them back toward Mercury. The ruse seemed to be working; Phantom was so distracted trying to maintain multiple fights, he didn't notice he was being corralled into submission.

*

Inside the house, Ethan, disguised as Grady, locked himself in the study to avoid being found before he could reconnect with his real body back in Nightmare's realm. A calm solitary quiet rested over him, and he considered the room with new eyes. Of course, this was just a dreamscape version and not really Grady's manor, but in the moment, the space seemed the same. He remembered the first time he'd ever entered the room, nervous but enchanted and completely oblivious to everything that would soon come afterward. He'd crossed a threshold that day without realizing, and here he was, crossing one again. At least this time, he was the one in control. Or, so he hoped.

He walked up to the large antique mirror that hung behind a bulky mahogany desk and Grady's visage looked back at him. He'd assumed being in someone else's body would feel weird, especially his boyfriend's, but he didn't feel any different from when he was in his own. Perhaps because this body was a dream version. Perhaps because he'd never completely been at home in his own body anyway.

Ethan, calm and feeling as in control of himself as ever, closed his eyes and imagined his true body as an anchor pulling him in. Grady wasn't there to call him back like before, but he believed he could do it himself now.

Sure enough, when he opened his eyes, he was himself again and back in Nightmare's realm. The only real surprise was that Nightmare had gone. A brief panic-stricken Ethan worried that he'd been duped, and Nightmare could be helping Phantom destroy his friends right at this very moment, but a quick mind-link to the others dispelled that fear. Nightmare wasn't in the dreamscape, and the others seemed to be doing just fine carrying on the ruse. Recalling Mercury's words, Ethan could only assume Nightmare had made himself scarce so he couldn't be accused of taking any sides.

Time to trap Phantom for good. Or at least, for another semi-eternity until he found some way to escape again.

Ethan focused again, mind-linking with the others. They had to die.

*

Successfully getting all the shadow demons within Mercury's reach, Grady watched from a short distance away as Mercury reformed them, and Phantom became himself again. Furious, he shapeshifted into a towering monster of night and terror, living up to his name.

"Children! Fools!" his voiced boomed across the dreamscape, causing a down burst of strong wind gusts to sweep through and whip around them. "You have yet to see true terror!"

A macabre whirlwind of gruesome figures made of shadows, and the dense black energy they'd seen in Nightmare's realm, formed in the sky like a twister of anguish and death on its way to consume them.

"I was beginning to wonder what made him so scary. Now I know," Marcus mused, impressed.

"Horror manifested," Grady, who still looked like Ethan, surmised. He was lucky he was talking to a ghost because otherwise the strong wind would have carried off his words for none to hear. "Imagine a scene like this on Earth."

"I have to admit, Hunter. Your boy is brilliant," Marcus conceded. "And I think I'm ready to make my exit from this little hellscape snow globe. Catch you on the other other side."

With a wink, Marcus disappeared.

"Bloody ghosts," Grady cursed. Although he knew his real body to be safe, his subconscious would still be trapped here until Ethan released them. He wished he'd hurry things up.

"I may not have Sandman," Phantom bellowed down from his lofty reign in the sky. He turned his large purpleorbed eyes on Mercury and what he assumed to be Ethan. "But I have the two of you, and I'm willing to experiment to see if the effects will be the same."

Phantom sent down a wrath of lightning alongside his tornado of twisted faces. Thankfully, it was precisely when Ethan called them back. The dream bodies of everyone else collapsed as though Phantom's attack had killed them all. Mercury was the only one, the only true body, left standing.

Phantom's lightning grin at his immediate destruction faded when he saw what he thought had been Ethan had died as well.

"What is this?" he demanded.

"I believe this is goodbye!" Mercury called up, appearing fresh and lively as ever. "You've got what you wanted. A world to rule over. Just with a small caveat: there are no subjects for you to terrorize. Minor details. We can't have everything, right?"

Realizing he'd been tricked, Phantom bellowed, which caused the whole dreamscape to vibrate and begin to crumble as he woke from the illusion. Ethan would need to seal the dreamscape up soon, so Mercury had to make a fast getaway.

"Family reunions are always so droll," Mercury said. "Let's not plan another one too soon."

Mercury transported himself back to Nightmare's realm, and Ethan rushed to seal his dreamscape, utilizing the oldest of Celestial magic. The dreamscape was now a locked bubble in a vast multiverse of piggybacking alternate realities and existed on the edge of Nightmare's realm for him to help watch over.

"Ethan, you are simply splendid. How did the universe ever function without you?" Mercury threw his arms around Ethan in a giant hug and kissed both of his cheeks in appreciation.

"I'm sure my father could've done better."

"Your father is glorious in his own right, but he was never much of a strategist. Speaking of Sandy, we should attend to him. He might need some help with the Elementals." Mercury smirked with amusement. "Sandboy doesn't work."

"What?"

"Well, we have to call you something," Mercury explained. "Having a Celestial named Ethan won't do. That's like having a constellation named Doug. '*At night, I stare up at the beautiful Doug in the sky.*' No. We'll call you the Dream Prince."

"Please don't. Plus, what if we find out there are more of us? I mean, for a while, they thought my father was the only one."

"Fine then. Something more suited to your specific talents." He thought some more and then snapped his fingers. "Dream Weaver! Yes. I like it. It implies you have more stories to tell, and I'm always looking forward to the next adventure."

Ethan grinned. "I can live with that."

Chapter Sixteen

A New Dawn Rises

Ethan grasped Grady tight as soon as he and Mercury arrived back in Kit's hut in the Dream World. The immense relief of the weight of worry lifted off his shoulders as he realized he could finally relax.

"We can't relax yet." Mercury seemed to cut through his thoughts deliberately. Probably so.

Still with arms wrapped around each other, Grady peered over Ethan's shoulder to ask, "Why? What on Earth could be happening now? I thought we'd secured Phantom."

"Earth is precisely where we're needed," Mercury said. "Phantom is secure, but Sandy and the techno-mage are up against a coven of Elementals. I feel the beckoning call of Death."

"Elementals?" Ethan hadn't been properly brought up to date. "What happened with the Order?"

"Don't worry about that." Mercury tried to get them to focus. "With Phantom out of the way, Vid dead, and Chase gone rogue, the Order is sufficiently defunct."

"Who?" Ethan furrowed his brow.

Mercury sighed.

Marcus chimed in. "Let's just say there are demigods of all sorts, and right now they're the ones winning. Chase is their leader. Chris built a device to try to stop him but has yet to implement it. Your father was transmutated into Sandman, and he and Chris are fighting the Elementals on their own as we speak."

"Thank you for translating," Mercury said.

Marcus shrugged. "You know I can be useful when I want to be."

"We have to help him!" Ethan insisted, full of renewed determination. Turns out beating a Celestial is quite a confidence booster.

Mercury rolled his eyes. "Is that not what I've been saying this whole time?"

As though he knew they were talking about him, Sandman arrived in an instant, appearing concerned and exhausted.

"We can't hold these guys on our own," he said. "How did things go with Phantom?"

"Ethan has him under lock and key, trapped in a dreamscape. Hopefully, for good," Mercury said with a proud smile.

Sandman swooped Ethan into his arms in a huge bear hug and kissed him on the top of his head with admiration.

Most likely overhearing the ruckus, Karen and Arthur appeared from a backroom of the hut.

"Vincent," Karen said in a surprised, breathy whisper.

Sandman addressed her with silent consideration.

Ethan intervened. "Mom, I know this might be confusing, but Dad isn't Dad anymore. This is Sandman. *The* Sandman."

Her eyes widened, brimming with tears.

"Such formalities!" Mercury apparently couldn't handle the awkward tension building in the room, nor the time they were wasting while Elementals rampaged on Earth. He walked up to take, what Ethan guessed had once been, his place beside Sandman. Mercury rested a hand on Sandman's shoulder, and Ethan couldn't help but notice Sandman leaned into the gesture.

With a triumphant grin, Mercury added, "Just call him Sandy."

"Do you retain any of my dad's memories?" Ethan asked, hopeful. "Like Mercury does with Dacey's?"

"The memories, yes," Sandman confirmed. "But my feelings are my own."

To demonstrate his meaning, he rested a hand over Mercury's, who still held fast to his shoulder.

Marcus grimaced but didn't seem compelled to say anything.

Perhaps because she'd already dealt with the loss before, Karen accepted the revelation with grace, and she shifted the conversation to her true priority.

"Where's Chris?"

"Acting as a lone soldier from what I can tell. He's all right but probably not for much longer." Mercury seemed lost in thought which meant he was using his celestial telepathic abilities to try to discern what was happening back on Earth.

"It must be quite a thing to have a crystal ball for a brain," Arthur stated in a most fascinated tone.

Mercury flashed a charming smile, but concern wore across his face. "Indeed, it is. And we really must go now. Don't worry, you two will be leaving this place soon. One way or another."

He disappeared, taking Sandman and Marcus with him.

"What's that supposed to mean?" Karen asked.

"He's Death. Better not to think about it." Arthur frowned.

Ethan tossed his hands up in the air. "Really? My own dad just leaves me to try to carry everyone by myself?"

"Perhaps Sandman and Mercury really are perfect for each other." Grady smirked at Ethan's plight. "I think we all have confidence that you're perfectly capable now."

Ethan realized he was right. After everything else, transporting others across realms was a cakewalk. In fact, he'd be lying to himself if he didn't admit he kind of liked showing off his abilities. To prove the point to himself, he proceeded to transport them all in an instant effortlessly.

*

As soon as the group was back on Earth, Ethan realized there was no time for clever ploys and strategies. The scene before them was an immediate call to action.

The Elementals had decided to test their strength out on the hometown of those they deemed the biggest nuisance. Downtown Shady Pines was already in shambles. The midcentury shops were beginning to crumble from bricks that had been knocked out of their structures, and some were on fire. Several cars were flipped over, and one pickup truck even hung upside down and halfway out of a bakery window. A large jackalope hopped through the street, stopping every now and then to munch flowers off the decorative bushes in front of restaurants.

Thankfully, it seemed as though most civilians were already taking shelter or had evacuated the area. Though, a few could be seen from various windows with their cameras out.

As Mercury had said, Ethan spotted Chris already fighting with a giant shadow man. The battle was more surreal than anything he could dream up.

"Everything we just pretended to do is happening for real now," Grady said.

Benny whimpered and he wasn't even in dog form. "I'm still exhausted from the warm-up."

Grady turned to Ethan with concern. "You should take Benny back to the Dream World with the others. He'll be safer there. If anything happened to him, this isn't a dream he'd be able to wake from with ease."

Ethan nodded in agreement and made the quick transport and drop-off before blipping right back to where he'd stood before.

"That was quick," Grady noted.

"This whole thing would be over a lot faster if I could create a temporal pause here, but that only works when I'm traveling," Ethan lamented.

"Doing so would render the rest of us relatively useless," Grady added.

"Except for Sandman," Ethan said.

Grady seemed to see where his thoughts were headed. "Any idea what effect a pause would have on the Elementals?"

"Not really," Ethan admitted. "Last time I did it, Mercury was with me in the Dream World. But...they come from a Celestial bloodline, but they're not technically full Celestials."

"We've made tough calls on less information before," Grady said. "I think it's at least worth a shot."

"I wonder..." Ethan had so many risky ideas now. He mind-linked with Mercury and Sandman.

I assume spirits can exist outside of time. Can I force someone to have an out-of-body experience?

I do love your imagination! Mercury responded. *And yes, I suppose if you tricked their subconscious into a state of lucid dreaming, then it would be entirely possible. What are you up to now, Dream Weaver?*

He told them his plan and instructed Sandman to do the same to Chris as he would do to Grady.

He then broke the mind-link and rested his hand on Grady's cheek with a gentle caress of his thumb.

"You're my anchor," Ethan reminded Grady, although it was more of a sentiment now. "I wouldn't want you to have to stay for this, but I need someone I can count on to make sure Chris's device can stop Chase. You're the only one I trust to see that through. If anything goes wrong—if you don't think you'll make it, call me back and I'll save you."

"You'd have to break the temporal pause to do that," Grady reminded him, although he knew that was the weight of what he'd be sacrificing.

"I know you think I'm some sort of moral compass, Grady. But none of us are perfect," Ethan admitted.

Protectiveness shone in Grady's gaze.

"Promise you'll call me back," Ethan insisted. "Don't go martyring yourself for the sake of my virtue. I've forgiven you for a lot of things, but I'd never forgive you for that."

Grady seemed as though he might cry, but he let out a small laugh instead. "You never have liked being thought of as the innocent one."

"Innocence is like time. An illusion that only means something if you want to believe it does."

Ethan kissed Grady as hard as he could as though the embrace might be their last. In that moment, he set Grady into a lucid dream state and left the Earth in limbo behind him.

*

Grady assumed he'd been knocked off his feet by the temporal shift. When he glanced down at his hands, they were as transparent as Marcus.

"Shit, I've died already."

"Simple O.B.E., dear heart." Mercury appeared by his side. "Don't tell me you've never had one before."

"There was a time once. But there were narcotics and witchcraft involved. It's all a bit fuzzy," Grady admitted.

"Well, keep your head clear this time because it looks like Ethan's idea just might work."

He was right. The chaos around them was frozen midaction. The only ones still moving around beside Mercury were Sandman, Marcus, the three nonhuman Elementals, Chris, and himself.

Chris also seemed to be having an out-of-body experience because he took long strides and floated in between like an astronaut enjoying the freedom from gravity.

"Is this what being a ghost is like? Because this is awesome!" Chris shouted.

"If you really think so, I'm sure we could help you along with the process," Marcus remarked with annoyance, obviously less enthusiastic about his gravity-free state.

"Help Chris get his restraining device on that rogue alchemist," Mercury instructed.

"All right, but then what do we do with him?" Grady wondered.

"The cosmos has taken prisoners before. He'll see the same treatment, I'm sure." Mercury gave a vague assurance. He then took off to help Sandman fight the other Elementals.

Due to the human blood flowing through his veins, Chase had been frozen in his rage. His body torqued to let loose another massive wall of fire. A faerie Elemental guarded him. Grady tried to think of a quick way to manipulate her into standing down but unfortunately Chris acted first.

"Look, lady, we don't want to fight with you," Chris said as they arrived in front of her, and she took a defensive stance. "Mostly because we all know we wouldn't win."

"Fuck's sake," Grady muttered.

"Great scare tactic." Marcus rolled his eyes.

She hadn't attacked them yet, so Chris ignored them and continued. "Just let us have the human flame thrower, and we can end this right now. We don't even have to hurt him."

"But we could, if that's a bargaining chip," Marcus chimed in.

Chris scowled at him.

"This is no mere human. He is a son of Dawn. The culmination of all Her glory. You're on the wrong side," the Elemental said. "He is bringing a new era. Humans, left unchecked, waste their time on this world, and its resources with their petty wars over chosen gods and imagined dominion. Gods they created, who never existed. Gods who abandoned them. They ignore the truth of the cosmos and kill everything around them with their inferior weapons and pollution. They had a chance once to change that, and they did not. The weak shall die, and the strong of heart shall be ushered forward under new laws. Chase represents their salvation. A world of half human, half elementals who will truly respect Dawn's creations. Don't you see? This is evolution. This is progress. Nothing stays as it is. Stand down and allow this changing of the guard. Welcome the son of Dawn as I have, and you might live to see the sunrise on a new and better world."

"A world that burns at his hands?" Marcus pointed out, indicating the fire-swept buildings around them.

"Destruction is nature's way to creation," she contended.

"While I am impressed by your very cult-like PSA and can't argue with the importance of environmental awareness, we would like to point out the flaw in your logic," Chris said and then turned to Grady, expectant. "Grady, why don't you enlighten her as to why letting Chase rule the world would be a bad idea?"

Shocked, and with nothing specific prepared to say, Grady froze in place much like the majority of everything else around them.

Chris moved his hand in a rolling hurry-up motion that made Grady realize his job wasn't to debate but to be a distraction.

Dick move, Grady thought but cleared his throat to perform. "Right. Uhm..."

Surprisingly, the faerie gave him her full attention, clearly intrigued at whatever he might say. Honestly, Grady wondered the same thing himself because he had no fucking clue what would come out of his mouth.

"The flaw, yes..." Grady hurried to attempt to put together something even remotely sensible. "Humans have caused a lot of destruction, you're right. But what I think you fail to see is just because we're human—"

Marcus cleared his throat, entirely for show since he no longer had the capability of doing the action for its natural purpose.

"Most of us, anyway," Grady amended if for no other reason than to buy time. He still had her attention, or so he thought. Her gaze seemed to settle just over his shoulder. "It doesn't mean you shouldn't throw our cautions aside. Your leader there…"

"Chase," Marcus offered.

"Chase is one of the most destructive humans," Grady jumped on the debate. "He may be a son of Dawn as you claim, but does that mean he's not capable of being flawed? How do you know he won't turn on you next?"

Her eyes widened. She shouted, "No!"

Surprised his terrible ploy had any effect whatsoever, especially such a drastic one, Grady made a quick effort to console her. "It's all right. We all make mistakes. You just have to change course—"

With fury, she conjured a down burst of wind that would've normally blown a man off his feet if he hadn't currently been the product of an out-of-body experience. She rushed away toward whatever had her attention.

Grady and Marcus glanced behind them to see Mercury had just killed the Shadow Man, and Sandman had put the jackalope into a deep state of sleep. "I don't think she was paying attention to your speech. Rousing though it may have been."

Grady sneered. "Thank you for that astoundingly helpful observation."

"Great job, guys!" Chris called, seeming unaware they'd done nothing useful. Sandman and Mercury appeared beside them while the faerie was preoccupied trying to revive the jackalope.

"Now let's just hope I'm as good at inventing weapons of mass distraction as we think." Chris, thankfully, showed no hesitation. He slapped the cuffs on Chase, and Grady cried out in pain. Everyone turned to look at him.

Not understanding where the sensation came from, Grady grabbed his torso, which wasn't effective at all since he currently appeared in spirit form.

Yet, somehow, dizziness began to consume him.

"Hunter, what's the matter with you?" Marcus was closest to him and seemed surprisingly concerned for once. Probably because ghosts shouldn't be able to feel pain. He added, "You don't look so well."

Grady knew he wasn't a ghost, though, and the pain in his chest became sharper. He, along with the others who had pieced things together, stared back at his physical body, which had been left behind on the sidewalk slumped by a tree.

The faerie Elemental stood above his body. Her arm, now a long branch, punctured through his chest.

"No," he gasped, not wanting to believe what was happening.

"Call Ethan back!" Mercury shouted at him before transporting himself beside the Elemental and attacking her from behind. He tore her body away from Grady's, and she turned to fight him.

Throwing all cosmic caution to the wind again, Mercury removed his gloves and punched a skeletal hand through her chest and ripped out her heart. She diffused into a million tiny balls of light and floated up toward the sky.

Grady could feel the tether to his physical body pulling him back. The pain a beckoning call.

Chris had already apprehended Chase. Grady knew Sandman still had the opportunity to transport Chase to another world or dreamscape during the pause, but if time resumed before that happened, then it might mean failure. However, if Grady drifted back inside his body before he could summon Ethan, then there'd be no telling how long he'd be stuck, wounded in the temporal pause, before Sandman or Mercury could call Ethan back themselves, and he was uncertain if that meant he could die frozen in a moment.

His moral dilemma aside, Ethan had given him clear instructions. And the last thing Grady wanted was to die and become Marcus's ghostly bosom buddy for the rest of eternity. As much as he suspected that would please Mercury.

Struggling to focus over the pain and disturbing pull of the tether, Grady called out to Ethan in his mind multiple times. He worried the anchor would be less effective with him in a spirit form, but once he snapped back into his own body, time resumed around him, and he knew he'd succeeded.

Spotting the blood-soaked ripped fabric of his shirt, Ethan fell to his knees beside Grady and grabbed hold of him. "No, no, no!"

"Ethan." Grady said out of breath.

"Please tell me you're not dying." Tears filled Ethan's eyes.

Grady gave a little smirk as he clutched the side of his chest. "I'm not dying. At the moment, anyway. Just a few broken ribs, I think."

Ethan let out a sigh of relief.

"I have an idea. Hang tight." Ethan disappeared.

"Hang tight?" Grady repeated to himself. "Mortally wounded and all my boyfriend says is 'Hang tight.'" He shook his head. "Americans."

In moments, Ethan returned with Vivian and Thomas at his side.

Grady spotted a vial of one of Vivian's healing potions in her hand.

"I don't know if that will be enough this time." Grady gritted his teeth through the pain.

"New blend," Ethan assured him. "Hope you don't mind being a test subject."

Ethan allowed Vivian to take some of his dream energy, which Grady knew would at least, thankfully, quell the sharp pain. She closed the vial with the dream energy swirling inside, blending with her usual concoction, and she chanted in a soft voice to the substance, coaxing the elixir into effectiveness.

Thomas stared down at him, his expression unreadable.

"I suppose you take some enjoyment in seeing me like this." Grady peered up at him.

"I wish I could," Thomas replied. "But it turns out there are worse people to concern myself with."

His eyes darted back to where they'd left Chase.

Eager to know how that was going as well, Grady drank the elixir as soon as Vivian offered the substance to him.

Feeling the healing effects beginning to work and the blissful absence of pain provided by Ethan's energy, Grady found his footing. He ripped his shirt off and allowed Vivian to bandage his chest. Thank goodness he had a friend who knew the importance of wielding witchcraft and first aid kits.

"Yes, this is much more what I remember an out-of-body experience feeling like." Grady gave a slight drugged smile to Mercury.

*

With Grady now safe in Vivian's company, Ethan took off to join Sandman who was now dealing with a reanimated Chase.

"What do you think you're doing?" Chase demanded as he failed one attempt after another of trying to produce the fire he once commanded. He banged his arms against a nearby mailbox in order to try to break free of the cuffs, but they remained intact.

"I hate to break it to you, Chase, but for once, you're completely normal," Chris explained. "Well, so to speak."

Infuriated, Chase lunged for Chris. "Your primitive contraptions won't hold me for long, mage!"

Sandman grabbed hold of him to protect Chris. Chase struggled, refusing to believe he'd been overpowered.

"Primitive?" Chris scoffed. "Seems pretty advanced to me."

"Your magic is ancient energy. Stolen energy!" Chase spat. "And you don't have the capacity to understand it."

Ethan stood in front of him, meeting his gaze. "It's time you left. For good. This universe doesn't need two Phantoms."

Chase sneered, and his lips twisted into an evil grin. "Phantom, like all creatures of the night, was a fool. A dreamer. Like you. All you can see are distortions of reality, whereas I know the truth. I harness the light. I see *everything*. Phantom proved to be nothing more than a precursor to a new day. Where I will—"

"Yeah, yeah. We already heard this speech from Goth Tinkerbell. Get him out of here." Chris signaled that Sandman was more than welcome to take him away.

"Do you want me to help you seal him in a dreamscape?" Ethan offered.

"Thanks, but I think I can handle this weasel. I'm partially responsible for this mess in the first place. I need to do my part to end this," Sandman assured him. He nodded back toward Grady and the others. "There are things here that need your attention."

"Dreamscape?" Chase's eyes widened.

Sandman gripped him by the collar now and squeezed tight. "That's right. Remember that little box you wanted to shove me in? It's like that. But I'll be sure to fill it with your worst nightmares."

Mercury fanned himself and whispered, "I always loved when he'd get like this."

"Trust me, Sandman. If you try to cross a veil with me, then I will be your worst nightmare," Chase dared him.

"Can it. I'm not wasting any more time on you," Sandman said.

Sensing an abundance of red flags from the pleased glint in Chase's eyes, Ethan tried to intervene. "Dad, I don't think—"

But Sandman transported them before Ethan could finish.

"Well, that's that." Chris brushed his hands together like dusting off a hard day's work.

The sky turned an opalescent purple, and lightning cracked in sideways bolts throughout the clouds in a web that seemed to sear through the atmosphere.

"If by 'that' you mean the beginning of an apocalypse, then yes, I suppose you're right." Mercury frowned, staring up at the sky just as disillusioned as the rest of them.

Grady and the others ran over to join the group, and Shady Pines residents who had been seeking shelter began to peek out from their hiding spots to get a better look at the lightning and firestorm brewing in the stratosphere.

"What's going on?" Ethan demanded of Mercury. "Did you know this would happen?"

"Of course not!" Mercury defended himself. "This is unprecedented. We're dealing with a nondream creature, half human, half Elemental transport from Earth into a Dream dimension. There's a strong chance things could have gone sideways! He could have—" Mercury's eyes widened at his own realization. "He could have transmutated during the process!"

A hot wind began to pick up around them.

"Dammit!" Chris ran his fingers through his spiky blue hair and tugged chunks in frustration. He seemed to be running a silent calculation. "Variables are a bitch!"

He was frantic, an apologetic frown plastered in place of his usually upbeat expression. "The restraints aren't going to work on a full Elemental in a subconscious realm. They rely on human life force and physical grounding. If Mercury's right, then even if Chase is still in his body, across the veil, his Elemental spirit has taken over as primary. It would render the device futile."

"What does that mean?" Ethan panicked.

"It means we just set a Fire Celestial free!" Chris answered.

As though highlighting his point, lightning cracked the sky again, but this time the bolts didn't fade away. They began to glow brighter until they were whips of fire racing across the sky.

"How do we stop him?" Ethan turned to Mercury who, up to this point, had seemed to have all the answers. He still did. It just wasn't the one he wanted to hear.

"We don't," Mercury admitted sadly. "We can't. This is beyond any one of our abilities. We'd need help from one of the Ancient Celestials, and they abandoned us long ago."

"What about combined abilities?" Ethan pressed. He wasn't taking no for an answer.

"I'm sorry, Dream Weaver." Mercury frowned. "Ethan...we've lost."

The sky began to drop flames like rain.

Ethan refused to accept what he was hearing. He would keep demanding answers until he got a useful one. "Is Sandman dead? You would sense it. You would know."

Mercury closed his eyes for a moment, focusing, then opened them again with relief. "He's still alive."

"Then we haven't lost yet," Ethan insisted. "We just need to contact an Ancient Celestial."

"Ethan! I can't believe you'd even suggest—" Mercury began a mild scandalized protest before Ethan could feel him reading his mind and then corrected course. "Oh, is that all? No, I don't think she'd listen."

"It's at least worth trying," Ethan pushed.

Sandman reappeared next to them. His clothes were charred, and he swatted out a few small flames that had been cascading up the front of his pants.

"Well that was a fucking disaster," he said, confirming their fears.

Grady spoke up. "Would you please be so kind as to enlighten us non-Celestial beings as to what you're talking about because I'm afraid we're all feeling rather out of the loop and understandably"—he pointed to the sky—"*doomed.*"

"Ethan is suggesting we tattle to Chase's mother," Mercury revealed. "Assuming, of course, she isn't the one who put him up to this in the first place."

"You want to bring Dawn into this?" Sandman seemed wary.

"If she's the one who put him up to this, then it doesn't change anything," Ethan persisted. "But if she didn't, then she's bound to know how to stop him. So, how do we summon Dawn?"

Chapter Seventeen

A Family Found

"You don't believe in pulling out, do you?" Mercury joked.

Ethan offered a cross expression. "Just summon her and hurry!"

Mercury sighed and took Sandman's hand in his. Ethan was correct. Dawn would be their best, and probably only, chance at overpowering her son. They'd never been certain of Dawn's motivations or intentions though. She had a murky past with them all.

Technically, if they left Earth to fall under Chase's reign, their small group could still survive in another world. However, if Dawn joined Chase in challenging them, then they were all walking into possible extinction.

But Mercury knew Ethan was more noble than even he would give himself credit for. He'd never accept the demise of his home world if there was even a remote chance they could still save it.

"Well, Sandy, I'm willing if you are. She's your relative, after all." He couldn't deny being overjoyed to touch him again. He could see from the adoration in Sandman's eyes he felt the same. Neither of them thought a reunion would ever be a possibility.

Things weren't quite the same though. In fact, everything was different. Except they were still pissing off other Celestials. Mercury smirked at that as he planted a deep kiss on Sandman's stardust lips.

The situation must have been too much for Marcus because he disappeared.

Sandman pulled him in closer, and Mercury wished this moment was leading to more than it was supposed to be.

The combined force of their Celestial energy coupled with their mental pleas for Dawn's attention worked faster than expected.

"Has everyone gone completely batshit?"

Mercury recognized her voice.

Dawn appeared as a radiant beacon of light, just as her name suggested. Her hair didn't only gleam in the sunlight—each strand was made of it, which is why the non-Celestials standing around were diverting their eyes. That or because she was very much naked. The Ancients, understandably, weren't too concerned with clothing. Mercury looked forward to such freedom again—once she obliged in helping them with the problem at hand.

"I know what you're thinking..." Sandman began.

"Unless you've somehow sucked Mercury's powers out through his lips, then I highly doubt that." Dawn crossed her arms.

The chaos churning in the sky caught her attention and took precedence. "Pretty certain that's not one of *my* weather patterns. I'll deal with you two in a moment."

Placing a hand on her hip and snapping her fingers, she invoked Chase back to Earth. He appeared human, but his eye sockets were glowing embers and heat could be seen radiating off his body.

The sky cleared up, minus a few scattered flames that were still left pouring down, and he stood in complete shock and confusion at her side.

"I always thought Tuft Stuff would be the problem child." Dawn shook her head and sighed like any overburdened mother. "I should have known. Fire Elementals. You're short tempered and shortsighted."

"Dawn," Chase muttered the realization aloud. He gave an awkward half bow, unsure of how to approach her. "Mother?"

She held her hand up to stop him. "Don't matronize me. I don't have time for traitors this millennia. You're grounded."

Snapping her fingers once more, Chase disappeared.

"What did you do to him?" Sandman asked.

Mercury whispered to Ethan, "Remember that little conversation we had about punishments from the gods?"

Ethan seemed to realize the power of the presence they were in.

"I converted him into something more useful," Dawn explained. "He'll live out the rest of his existence as a volcano in Albay. Trust me, this isn't the first time a son of mine has ended up in the magma trade. Now, would you care to explain why and *how* exactly the two of you found your way back to each other?"

*

While Sandman and Mercury filled her in on everything that had transpired, Ethan woke the jackalope from his dreamspell-induced slumber and let him run back to Dawn's side.

Ethan also took the opportunity to transport Karen, Arthur, and Benny back to Earth from the Dream World.

Karen ran to Chris, and he scooped her off her feet, twirling her around in a way Ethan had only seen in movies. It had taken stopping an apocalypse together, but Ethan would be happy to consider Chris family.

Once Dawn had been caught up, Ethan noticed she not only seemed surprised at the unforeseen turn of events but appeared impressed by him. She considered Ethan for the first time in earnest, and her gaze, while regal and stoic, was also filled with curiosity.

"Perhaps there is hope for the multiverse yet," she said. The simple sentence conjured a dozen new questions for Ethan, but she didn't elaborate, and he was too exhausted to even ask. If there were more fights headed his way in the future, he wasn't ready to know about them yet.

"Stay vigilant," she cautioned. "I'm certain this will not be the last of Phantom's tricks. And I will keep a closer eye than I have been on the rest of my children."

She placed a protective hand on Tuft Stuff, who twitched his nose and nuzzled up against her.

"There are more of them?" Ethan shuddered.

Her telling smile made him certain there were many more.

"They're not all bad." But that was all she let on before correcting all of Chase's destruction. She then disappeared, taking the jackalope with her.

"I witnessed all of that with my own eyes, and I still don't believe it," Chris said.

Grady breathed a sigh of relief. "I can't believe we're still alive."

"You, especially," Thomas remarked, gesturing to Grady's wound. Thanks to Vivian's concoction, he must have forgotten with everything else because he suddenly clasped his hand to his side again as though he just remembered he wasn't bulletproof.

Ethan turned to Mercury. "Where's Marcus?"

"Sulking in the Spirit World, I'm sure." Mercury wore a sympathetic smirk, "He'll get over it soon enough."

"C'mon. We're not finished with this mess yet," Sandman said, nodding toward the onlookers, who had made their way out into the street. He gestured for Ethan to help him.

Following his lead, Ethan helped his father weave through the crowds and replace their memories with false ones to erase everything they'd seen. For them, they'd remember this day as just another ordinary one with maybe a few strange daydreams.

*

Grady had suggested they all get out of the public eye as soon as possible and led them back to his manor. After a vivacious greeting from the housekeeping ghosts, Agatha and John, and a well-check on Grady's rapid healing injury, they were all resting in the still unruly-from-battle study. Some, such as Mercury, were conversing as though it were any ordinary day while others wore expressions of traumatic exhaustion.

Grady drank the tea Agatha had provided them all upon their arrival in what seemed to be one gulp. Seeing the damage around the house, he realized things weren't quite settled in his mind, and he still had one more gigantic thing he'd like to tackle today.

He turned to Ethan, who stood beside him staring at the room full of friends and family with a dreamy expression. No doubt it was a sight he'd never expected to see in his life. His past and present colliding into a future he'd never imagined possible.

"Ethan, I—" Grady began but stopped short as Sandman approached them.

"I'm heading back to the Dream World," Sandman said. "There's still a lot of work ahead of me there, and I have some unfinished business to attend to with Nightmare."

"At least now I can see you any time I want...Dad." Ethan smiled awkwardly as though the idea was still settling in.

Sandman hugged him tight. "I'm so proud of you. And I look forward to getting to know more about you."

"What a lovely scene of familial bliss!" Mercury stated as he and Marcus—indeed over his sulking—joined them. "And, Dream Weaver, you were every bit as amazing as I knew you would be. Completely worth every pain in the ass on my multi-lifelong journey to get to this point."

"Dream Weaver?" Marcus raised an eyebrow.

"Yes, that's his nickname now," Mercury whispered over his shoulder to his ghostly tagalong. "I gave it to him."

Marcus harrumphed.

Addressing the others again, Mercury continued, "We must also take our leave back to the Spirit World. But first, I'd like you to bear witness to a passing of the torch."

He turned to the ghost floating beside him. "Marcus. My lover, my companion. We've been through so much together. Not all good, obviously. You were atrocious at times."

Marcus frowned.

Mercury went on. "But I can't imagine existing without you, and let's be honest, you'll never quit haunting me anyway. So, why don't we make this thing official? Until I was forced to wear two hats, I always worked alongside Death as his messenger. There's been a job opening for a while, so..." He removed his cloak and gestured for Marcus to wear the garment.

Marcus took the cloak with reluctant confusion. "You want me to take over as Death?"

"Certainly not!" Mercury laughed with such a high pitch his voice chimed. "Can you imagine the horrors you'd invoke? Oh my, no. But Death does need a messenger, and I can't imagine anyone else I'd like at my side for eternity."

Marcus appeared dumbfounded as he slid the cloak on. His ghostly visage transformed back into his former state. Relieved to feel somewhat himself again, Marcus smiled for once and gave Mercury his genuine respect. "Thank you."

"Of course, darling. Just don't go causing random plagues every time you lose your temper, and everything should all work out just fine."

Grady seemed unnerved by the prospect and leaned forward to whisper to Mercury. "Are you sure that's a good idea?"

Mercury smirked and whispered back, "My dear, there are no such things as good ideas. Only big or small ones, and we both know my preference on that." He winked.

Turning his attention back to Ethan and Sandman, Mercury added, "I'm certain we'll see one another soon. Until then, I leave the subconscious realm of this world in your more than capable starlit hands. *Au revoir*, darlings."

He gave them each a kiss on the cheek; the one planted on Sandman's lingered just ever so much longer. Then he and Marcus disappeared.

"Well, I can only hope I made it to Marcus's good side, or else I'm certain he'll convince Mercury to have me drop dead any moment now," Grady jested, prompting a chuckle from Ethan.

Sandman smiled. "On that note, I'll say goodbye as well." He glanced over his shoulder at the lounge chair where Karen and Chris sat together and offered them a small wave of farewell. With kind smiles, they returned the gesture.

"Wait!" Benny ran over to Sandman, tripping over his own feet in an effort not to miss him. "I want to go with you."

"What?" Grady and Ethan shared unified surprise.

Benny tried to find a gentle way to phrase his decision. "Well... I mean... I would miss you guys. But like Ethan said, you can travel to the Dream World whenever you want. So, it's not like I'd never get to see you again. Plus, there's just not really anything here for me. I mean, I'll miss taco shops, all-you-can-eat buffets, binge watching shows on Animal Planet, chew toys—"

"Benny," Ethan prodded him to focus as the list appeared to be endless.

Benny shored things up. "What I'm trying to say is, you guys have each other and I'd like that too. I mean, I think I've found that. There, with someone. In the Dream World."

Grady smiled, happy for his part-time four-legged friend as he realized what he was on about. "Kit?"

Benny shook his head with such glee the motion pretty much equated to him wagging his tail.

"You deserve to be happy." Grady patted him on the shoulder. "That's all I ever really wanted for you anyway. So, I don't see why not. As long as that's all right with Sandman."

"Of course," Sandman agreed. "Have you ever seen Canis Major? Celestials adore dogs. You'll fit right in. And, just between us, I know Kit pretty well, and I can tell she adores you too."

Benny was so overjoyed his wide eyes seemed like they might explode.

"One last thing," Sandman said. He handed the Codex over to Ethan. "This belongs to you now. Make good use of it."

"I will," Ethan said with appreciation.

"See you on the other side, son." Sandman smiled at Ethan. He nodded a goodbye to Grady and then disappeared, taking Benny.

"We save the world, and now everyone is looking for an excuse to leave it," Ethan mused as they now stood alone on their side of the room.

"Including myself," Grady let on, finally able to seize an opportunity to speak his mind.

"What?" Ethan faced him with curious surprise.

"It's a bit like Benny said," Grady explained, turning to Ethan with purpose. "There's nothing here for me anymore. Dr. Grady Hunter was a man who hunted and tamed supernaturals out of a sense of revenge and ignorant self-righteousness. This house, this world, was his life. But you're my life now—this man I've become. I told you in the past my real name was Alexander Quinn. I have no idea what name I should go by now, but what I do know more than any other fact is that I want to spend the rest of my life at your side. There's an entire multiverse out there, and I want to make it *our* home if you'll allow it."

Grady got down on his knee, taking Ethan's hands in his. "Ethan Roam, you're the only dream I've ever really wanted to come true. Will you marry me?"

The others in the room had grown silent, no doubt listening in as evidenced by occasional audible gasps of excitement.

As enthusiastic as they were, none of their reactions mattered to Grady. He only cared for the reaction of one person. The man he loved. And, to his relief, Ethan beamed at him.

"Yes," Ethan answered. "Of course, yes!"

Overjoyed, Grady stood and embraced him. He'd never had a kiss more electrifying than this one, and the sensation wasn't just because Ethan radiated pure dream energy.

A round of applause sounded from the others, and they all began to make their way over to congratulate them.

"One question." Ethan bit his lip in a precocious way. "About the name. How does Grady Roam sound?"

Grady's eyes welled with the warmth of joyous tears. "Heavenly."

"I'm so happy for you two!" Karen wrapped her arms around them in an excited group hug.

"I knew nothing would be able to keep you crazy kids apart! Not even an apocalypse," Chris teased. He slapped a congratulatory pat on Grady's back.

"Well, it sounds like I won't be around here much anymore." Grady faced them all as a group. "I guess I can't run a business. Perhaps I'll leave that to Vivian and Thomas to do with what they will? Vivian, you were always the one who the clients liked best anyway. And Thomas, maybe you can find a way to use your veterinary training to help some of the furrier supernaturals? The office still needs a doctor. A real one might be a good change of pace."

Thomas's jaw dropped, and Vivian hugged him tight. "Thank you! Oh, my goodness, thank you so much!"

Grady grinned to show her his admiration before continuing. "And, I suppose it's a bit silly to own a gigantic house I won't even be living in most of the time. Would the two of you like to stake your claim?" He raised his eyebrows generously at Karen and Chris.

"What?" Karen covered her mouth, floored. She shook her head. "No. We can't accept. It's too much."

"I don't know. I mean, *I* could accept it," Chris joked.

"Well, if you won't accept it outright, then at least accept the offer of becoming this place's live-in caretakers," Grady amended. "Agatha and John do all right but there are just some aspects of domestic responsibility that are better left to the living."

Karen, clearly emotional, nodded with deep appreciation. "Yes, I think we can handle that."

"Kind of weird to have your guy friend asking your girlfriend to move in with you *for* you and into not *your* place but *his*. But, whatever, I'm in." Chris grinned, giving a thumbs up and a wink.

"Fantastic, that just leaves Arthur." Grady turned to his old friend.

"Don't worry about me," Arthur smiled. "I've had more than enough excitement in my life thanks to you. In fact, enough to write another book. I'll be fine."

Grady smiled, at total ease for once in his life. "Everything is settled then. Alert the *Gazette*. Dr. Grady Hunter has officially left Shady Pines. And Ethan Roam is marrying some English prat nobody has ever heard of."

Ethan laughed. Grady took his hand again, and they weaved their fingers together in blissful unity.

*

The sun had set, and a quiet calm rested over Shady Pines. Everyone had left Grady's manor to attend to their personal business and rest. Vivian and Thomas were going to spend the next week moving back to Shady Pines, so they could start fresh as the new owners of the Alternative Healing Clinic. Karen and Chris would return in a couple of days to begin the process of taking over the household management, including helping Grady convince Agatha and John the change wouldn't be the end of the world. They'd already circumvented that. With Benny now in the Dream World, Grady and Ethan had the manor all to themselves.

A knife on the floor caught Ethan's eye as they surveyed the mess remaining in the study from the Order's ambush before Ethan had successfully transported everyone to safety in the Dream World for the first time.

Ethan picked the blade up and felt the weight of the hilt in his palm. It was the same knife he'd borrowed to protect himself the first night he'd stayed in Grady's home.

"It's crazy to think I only just showed up here a few months ago with no idea at all of what a sandman really was or that I'd end up being one," he mused.

"I'm finding it's crazy to think about most anything these days." Grady offered a supportive smile. "But at least we can relax now knowing the worst is behind us."

"I hope so," Ethan said. *Perhaps there is hope for the multiverse yet.* Dawn's odd statement weighed on him. He placed the knife back on the antique weaponry table where it belonged.

Grady must have been able to sense his unease. "Something on your mind?"

Ethan put on a brave face, not wanting to entertain thoughts of any more danger. "No. I've just learned you have to accept you can never really be sure of anything. The good, the bad. Dreams and nightmares. You have to expect it all, but also take everything in stride."

Grady nodded in silent agreement. He took one last survey of the mess around them and must have decided the disarray wasn't worth his worry because he chose to make his way across the room. They were now side by side behind the lounge chair that faced the fireplace.

"Speaking of that... *Dream Weaver*," Grady teased. "As eager as I am to see everything that exists in the conscious and subconscious realms, I hope maybe we could take advantage of the couple nights we might have alone here. Really let Shady Pines give us the send-off we deserve."

Ethan chuckled. "What do you suggest? Track a few vampires? Annoy a few witches? Pay a visit to that banshee, Wailing Walter?"

Grady narrowed his eyes and smirked. "I will be *so* glad to leave Vivian to have to deal with Walter. No." He gave Ethan a gentle tap on his chest near his heart. "I know you know perfectly well what I mean."

Grady wrapped his arms around Ethan's waist and pulled him close. "I want all the sandman tricks."

Ethan smiled, glad to know Grady could still make him blush.

"How about we start with this one?" Ethan said. He flicked his hand at the large mirror above the fireplace and it morphed into a window that contained an infinite universe. Stars began to float out of the frame and into the room to surround them, sweeping them both off their feet. As they hovered, Ethan's body morphed into his sandman form, and he kissed Grady, touching their tongues together and transferred dream energy into him. The effect was surreal bliss.

When their lips eventually parted, Grady said in an elated whisper, "If that's just the introduction, I can't wait for the showstopper."

Ethan returned everything to its normal state, including their feet meeting the floor once again.

"Oh, I have so many tricks you haven't seen yet," Ethan boasted seductively. "But I have an idea for a better stage."

"You read my mind," Grady agreed as they walked out of the study, arms around each other. "You're not telepathic now too, are you?" he teased one last time.

Ethan grinned. "No. Just very empathetic."

As Ethan turned to shut the door, he swore a face in the mirror stared out at them, but the visage disappeared like a phantom trapped inside.

A chill ran down his spine. Unaware of what he'd just witnessed, Grady ran his hand in a tender motion up Ethan's back, guiding him away from the room.

Ethan forced himself to push down the terrible thoughts creeping up. He knew now that life would continue to find ways to test him. There would always be another nightmare to face and creatures bigger than himself to contend with.

But Grady had shown him so long as he believed in his own power and perseverance, he could handle anything that came his way.

For now, he'd much rather focus on the present and the potential lifetime of traveling to new realms with the man he loved.

He'd learned each new dawn could be conquered by remembering he only had to make it through the night.

Epilogue

"Is this what you'd imagined?" Ethan asked.

He'd transported them into a dreamscape of desert-like conditions. There were minimal surroundings, and what few plants existed appeared as though they might be melting under a nonexistent sun. A gigantic glowing moon hung over their heads, seeming to threaten to fall out of the sky and start bouncing around them.

Grady seemed a little unsettled, though impressed. Ethan knew Grady had thought they'd be headed for the bedroom, but this opportunity had been too enticing to pass up.

"I think perhaps I expected something more...intimate," Grady said. A small clock with the legs of a chicken passed by them on its way to a small pond that might have been a mirage.

"And assuredly less disconcerting," Grady added.

Ethan laughed. "Okay, I think I know just the thing."

The dreamscape morphed into a dark galaxy of neon shooting stars. Just as Grady jumped, fearful of a possible falling sensation, Ethan formed a giant cotton-candy-pink cloud beneath them. They were all alone, floating along in a vast universe.

Ethan slid his arms through Grady's from behind and rested his chin on Grady's shoulder as his fiancé stared, awestruck, at the beauty surrounding them.

"Better?" Ethan whispered into his ear.

"Infinitely."

He could hear the smile in Grady's voice.

Grady turned to face him and discovered Ethan commanded *everything* about their environment, including whether they were dressed. They were not.

"Can you control me here too?" Grady asked.

"No." Ethan smiled, though he had to admit the idea appealed to him. "But something tells me you'll do what I want anyway."

Ethan pulled him down so they could lay together in the soft wisps of cloud.

Grady grinned. "I bet I can guess what that *something* is." He kissed Ethan with loving force, pressing into him.

Ethan produced seductive murmurs between kisses, unable to hold back his own arousal. He transformed into his sandman appearance.

Grady pulled back but not out of surprise. His gaze conveyed love.

"Can we stay here like this forever?" The question sounded like a plea.

"No," Ethan admitted. He ran his fingers through Grady's short blond wavy hair. "But we can come here as often as we like. This will be our private getaway."

"How did I ever get so lucky?" Grady asked.

Ethan answered anyway. "Because you never gave up."

"Of course, I'd never give up on you." Grady smirked as though it were out of the question.

Ethan gave him a gentle smile. "I meant because you never gave up on yourself."

Grady paused as the words registered, and Ethan noticed something change within him. For the first time since he'd known him, Grady relaxed.

Ethan pulled him back down and planted gentle kisses on his lips, then neck, and down his chest. He kissed every inch of Grady he could, as though they had all the time in the world together because...they did.

About the Author

Dez Schwartz is a Dreampunk, Paranormal, & Gay Romance author.

Dez's longtime love of the paranormal, humor, and gay literary fiction inspired her to begin writing all the stories she wished existed. Her books are usually about dapper occultists, scheming supernaturals, ghost hunters, and gay romance.

When she's not passionately crafting tales, she can be found drawing, fawning over animals, or traveling with loved ones.

Email: dezschwartzauthor@gmail.com

Facebook: www.facebook.com/DezSchwartz

Twitter: @dez_schwartz

Website: www.dezschwartz.com

Other NineStar books by this author

Roam

Hunter

Also Available from NineStar Press

Connect with NineStar Press

www.ninestarpress.com

www.facebook.com/ninestarpress

www.facebook.com/groups/NineStarNiche

www.twitter.com/ninestarpress

www.tumblr.com/blog/ninestarpress

www.ingramcontent.com/pod-product-compliance
Lightning Source LLC
Chambersburg PA
CBHW050530190726
48284CB00003B/1014